The Dawn of the Jaguar

Anupam Roy

Published by Anupam Roy, 2024.

This is a work of fiction. Similarities to real people, places, or events are entirely coincidental.

THE DAWN OF THE JAGUAR

First edition. October 7, 2024.

Copyright © 2024 Anupam Roy.

ISBN: 979-8227149503

Written by Anupam Roy.

Table of Contents

Preface 1
Chapter 1: The Flames of Prophecy 5
Chapter 2: The Gift of Sight 11
Chapter 3: The Jaguar's Warning 17
Chapter 4: Shadows in the Court of Yax Mutal 25
Chapter 5: The Flames of Fate 29
Chapter 6: The Meeting of Fate 35
Chapter 7: Shadows of Doubt 41
Chapter 8: The Flight into the Jungle 47
Chapter 9: Trials of the Jungle 53
Chapter 10: Shadows in the Palace 59
Chapter 11: The Battle at the Sacred Cenote 65
Chapter 12: Into the Waters of Destiny 71
Chapter 13: Return to a City on the Brink 77
Chapter 14: The Gathering Storm 81
Chapter 15: The Breaking of Blood 87
Chapter 16: The Siege of Yax Mutal 93
Chapter 17: Signs from the Sky 99
Chapter 18: Brothers at War 105
Chapter 19: Visions of Destruction and Hope 111
Chapter 20: The Breaking of the Bloodline 115
Chapter 21: The Jaguar's Summoning 119
Chapter 22: The Jaguar's Price 125
Chapter 23: The Crown and the Curse 131
Chapter 24: The Final Vision 135
Chapter 25: The King's Farewell 141
Chapter 26: The Final Offering 147
Chapter 27: Shadows of the Past 151
Chapter 28: The Weight of Peace 157
Chapter 29: The Eternal Guardian 161
Chapter 30: A New Dawn 165

Preface

In the heart of the dense Mesoamerican jungles, the ancient Maya civilization once flourished—its pyramids rising high toward the heavens, its cities teeming with life, ritual, and the ever-watchful gaze of the gods. For centuries, the Maya people stood as one of the most advanced and enigmatic cultures of the ancient world. Their knowledge of the stars, mathematics, and time itself was unparalleled, but beneath this grandeur lay a complex world of political intrigue, spiritual devotion, and constant war.

The Dawn of the Jaguar is a story set in the late Classic Period of this great civilization, a time when cities like Yax Mutal (known today as Tikal) and Calakmul were locked in an endless struggle for power. It is a tale of kings and commoners, of warriors and prophets, and of the delicate balance between the human and the divine. At its heart is the story of two individuals—Ixchel, a village girl with a mysterious gift, and Balam, a prince caught between his duty and his destiny. Their journey, set against the backdrop of the fall and rise of empires, explores the timeless themes of sacrifice, leadership, and the price of peace.

In writing this story, I have tried to capture not only the vibrant world of the Maya but also the spiritual weight that shaped their lives. The gods were not distant figures, but ever-present forces, deeply involved in the fate of their people. It is through this lens that *The Dawn of the Jaguar* unfolds, where every choice, every sacrifice, ripples through both the human and divine realms.

This book is both a tribute to the mysteries of the ancient Maya and a meditation on the choices we all face in times of great conflict. What does it mean to lead? To follow? To sacrifice for a future that may not come in our lifetime?

ANUPAM ROY

I hope you will find yourself immersed in the world of Yax Mutal, walking its stone streets, standing before its towering pyramids, and feeling the weight of destiny upon your shoulders as Ixchel and Balam did. Together, they remind us that sometimes, it is only through sacrifice that we find salvation—and only through struggle that we truly understand the dawn of a new era.

Welcome to *The Dawn of the Jaguar*.

— Anupam Roy

THE DAWN OF THE JAGUAR

ANUPAM ROY

Chapter 1: The Flames of Prophecy

The sun hovered low in the sky, casting a golden glow over the city of Yax Mutal. The city, known for its towering pyramids and intricately carved temples, buzzed with the energy of preparation. It was the day of a great ritual—one that would call upon the favor of the gods and ensure the continued prosperity of the kingdom. All paths led toward the *Temple of the Great Jaguar*, its stone facade gleaming under the fading light, adorned with banners and sacred offerings.

Among the crowds that gathered to witness the ceremony, a young girl named *Ixchel* stood at the edge, clutching her shawl tight around her shoulders. She was not from Yax Mutal; her family hailed from a small village nestled in the hills just beyond the city's borders. They rarely came to the capital, but today was an exception. The king himself, *Jasaw Chan K'awiil I*, would preside over the ceremony, calling upon the gods for protection against the rising tides of war and famine.

Ixchel's mother, *Itzel*, stood beside her, her face awash with awe as she stared up at the grand temple. "Look, Ixchel," her mother whispered, her voice trembling with reverence. "This is a sight we may never see again in our lives."

But Ixchel could not share in her mother's excitement. There was a tension in the air, one that pressed against her skin like an unseen force. The city was too loud, too crowded. The towering pyramids felt suffocating. Something was wrong, though she couldn't yet put her finger on it.

"Come," her father, *Ahau*, said, his voice a deep rumble, "the ceremony is starting."

They moved with the crowd toward the center of the plaza, where thousands of people had already gathered. The beating of drums echoed through the stone streets, their rhythm slow and purposeful, like the heart of the city itself. Priests clad in elaborate headdresses and flowing robes lined the steps of the pyramid, chanting in an ancient tongue that vibrated in the air.

At the peak of the pyramid stood King Jasaw Chan K'awiil I, tall and imposing, his face stern with the weight of leadership. Beside him, high priests prepared the sacred objects: jade statues, incense burners, and vessels of blood offered to the gods in ritual sacrifice.

As the sun dipped below the horizon, the king raised his arms, and a hush fell over the crowd. The sky shifted from gold to a deep crimson, and the torches lining the temple steps flickered to life, casting long shadows across the stone.

"The gods have blessed us with life," the king's voice boomed, carrying over the plaza. "But we must honor them. We must give in return to receive their favor."

Ixchel's heart pounded in her chest. There was an eerie stillness now, as if the entire world were holding its breath. She glanced around, her eyes wide, feeling something stir deep within her. The jaguar carvings on the temple seemed to shimmer in the flickering light, their stone eyes glowing with a strange, unnatural light.

She could barely hear her mother's soft prayers beside her. All her attention was on the jaguar faces—carved into the very walls of the pyramid. Their sleek forms seemed to ripple and shift under the flame's dance. Ixchel blinked, telling herself it was a trick of the light, but the tension in her chest grew unbearable.

"The gods demand a sign," the king's voice rang out again.

Suddenly, Ixchel felt as though the ground beneath her feet shifted. She stumbled, grabbing onto her father's arm for balance. But no one else seemed to notice. They were all too focused on the ritual unfolding before them.

The priests began their chants again, lower and more rhythmic this time. A group of dancers appeared, their steps mimicking the sleek movements of a jaguar stalking its prey. Ixchel's breath quickened, and a strange dizziness overtook her.

And then, the vision hit.

It began as a whisper at the edge of her mind, a dark presence creeping in like a shadow. Ixchel gasped, her knees buckling, and for a moment, she was no longer standing in the plaza but in a darkened jungle. The sounds of the ceremony faded, replaced by the heavy, rhythmic thudding of drums that pounded in her ears. She turned, heart racing, and there, emerging from the trees, was a jaguar.

But it was no ordinary jaguar. It was massive, its eyes glowing with an unnatural, fiery light. Smoke curled from its mouth, and flames licked its sleek black fur as it stalked toward her. The heat was intense, suffocating, and with every step the jaguar took, the jungle around her ignited.

The ground trembled beneath her as the creature drew closer, its gaze locked onto hers. The world burned around her, the flames consuming everything in their path, swallowing the trees, the sky, and the city of Yax Mutal itself. The great pyramids crumbled into ash, and the screams of the people filled her ears, echoing in the distance.

"Ixchel!"

Her mother's voice cut through the vision, and Ixchel gasped, her eyes flying open. She was back in the plaza, but her body trembled, her skin slick with sweat. Her mother knelt beside her, gripping her arms, her face pale with fear.

"Ixchel, what's wrong?"

"I—" Ixchel tried to speak, but her throat was dry, her voice strangled. She looked up at the temple, expecting to see the jaguar emerging, but there was nothing there. Yet, the vision was so vivid, so real, that her heart still raced in her chest.

Her father's deep voice rumbled beside her. "She's unwell. The heat, perhaps. Come, we should go."

"No," Ixchel protested weakly, her mind still reeling. "I... I saw something. The city... it was burning."

Her mother exchanged a worried glance with her father. "It was just a dream, child. The heat and excitement—"

"It wasn't a dream!" Ixchel's voice broke, drawing the attention of those around her. She shrank back, her hands gripping her shawl as she lowered her voice. "It wasn't a dream. I saw it. The jaguar... it will destroy the city."

Her father frowned. "Ixchel, enough. You're scaring your mother."

But her mother's eyes had already darkened with concern. She knew about Ixchel's visions—had seen them since she was a child, though they had never been so intense, never so terrifying.

The ceremony continued around them, the king's voice echoing once more across the plaza as he called upon the gods for protection and strength. The people of Yax Mutal cheered and raised their arms in unison, chanting prayers to the heavens. But to Ixchel, their voices felt distant, drowned out by the lingering image of the burning city in her mind.

She stood there, frozen, her gaze fixed on the temple. The jaguar gods carved into its walls seemed to stare back at her, their stone faces unblinking and eternal. Her heart thundered in her chest, a deep, primal fear rising within her.

The flames. The jaguar. The end of Yax Mutal.

Ixchel could not shake the feeling that something terrible was coming, something beyond the power of the king or his priests to stop.

She turned to her mother, her voice trembling. "We need to leave. We need to warn someone."

But before her mother could respond, a hand clamped down on her shoulder. It was one of the city guards, his face impassive as he looked down at her.

"The king summons you."

THE DAWN OF THE JAGUAR

And thus, Ixchel's life, once quiet and unknown, was about to change forever.

Chapter 2: The Gift of Sight

The quiet of the early morning was interrupted by the soft cooing of birds and the gentle rustle of leaves in the wind. Ixchel sat by the river near her family's small home, knees pulled up to her chest, staring at her reflection in the water. Her dark hair hung loose over her shoulders, and her eyes, though young, seemed heavy with a burden far beyond her years.

Since the ceremony in Yax Mutal, the vision of the jaguar and the flames had haunted her, flashing before her eyes every time she closed them. She tried to push it away, to convince herself it had been nothing more than a strange dream, brought on by the heat and excitement. But deep down, she knew it was more than that. The gods had spoken to her. The jaguar was real.

"Ixchel," a soft voice called from behind her. It was her mother, Itzel, her brow furrowed with concern as she approached. "Come inside, child. You'll catch a chill out here."

Reluctantly, Ixchel rose, her fingers still trembling slightly as she followed her mother back to their modest home—a small hut made of wood and thatch, with a fire pit in the center that warmed the room on cool mornings. Her father, Ahau, was already up, sharpening his tools for the day's work.

"You were out by the river again," he remarked without looking up, his tone gentle but stern. "You need to rest, Ixchel. You've been restless since we returned from Yax Mutal."

Ixchel opened her mouth to respond, but the words caught in her throat. She hadn't told them everything about the vision yet, only that she had felt strange during the ceremony. Her father, always practical, wouldn't understand. He would brush it off as an overactive imagination. But her mother... her mother would know.

Itzel sat down beside her, smoothing a hand over Ixchel's hair. "Tell us, my daughter," she said softly. "Tell us what troubles you."

For a moment, Ixchel hesitated. She didn't want to frighten her mother or anger her father. But she couldn't keep it inside any longer. She took a deep breath and began.

"It wasn't just the heat," Ixchel said, her voice barely above a whisper. "At the ceremony, I saw something. I saw the jaguar god. It was... it was more than a dream. The city—Yax Mutal—it was burning. The pyramids turned to ash, the people were screaming. The jaguar... it was in flames."

Her father paused, the sharpening stone still in his hand. His face remained calm, but there was a subtle tightening in his jaw. He was a man who believed in hard work, in things he could see and touch. Visions of gods and prophecies were things for priests, not farmers.

"You've always had strange dreams, Ixchel," Ahau said carefully. "But dreams are not the same as reality."

"It wasn't just a dream," Ixchel insisted, her voice rising slightly. "I felt it. I *saw* it. The city will burn. The jaguar god is coming."

Her mother's face grew pale, her eyes widening as she clasped Ixchel's hands tightly. "The gods have chosen you," she murmured, almost to herself. "I knew it. Since you were a child, I knew there was something special about you. The visions... they're a sign."

Ahau frowned, his grip tightening on the stone. "Itzel, don't encourage this. She's just a girl. She doesn't need to carry the weight of these... visions."

"But they've been happening for years," Ixchel said quietly, glancing between her parents. "Ever since I was little. I used to dream of things before they happened. When the rains came early last season, I saw it in a dream the night before. And when the crops failed the year before... I saw the drought coming too."

THE DAWN OF THE JAGUAR

Ahau sighed, setting his tools aside and rubbing a hand over his face. "That doesn't mean she's been chosen by the gods. Dreams, coincidences... these things happen."

"It's more than that, Ahau," Itzel said, her voice trembling with conviction. "I've seen it too. The way she knows things before they happen. The way the animals act around her, as if they understand her. Ixchel has a gift."

"A gift," Ahau echoed, his tone skeptical. "Or a curse."

There was a heavy silence that hung in the air after those words. Ixchel could feel her heart pounding, uncertainty gnawing at her. What if her father was right? What if these visions were not a blessing but a warning of something terrible?

Finally, her mother spoke again, her voice soft but firm. "We should speak to the priest, *Ah Kin Chi*. He's wise in the ways of the gods. He will know what to do."

Ahau shook his head. "The priests are busy with the city's troubles. They don't need to be bothered with the dreams of a child."

"She's no ordinary child," Itzel insisted. "The gods have chosen her. You'll see. Ah Kin Chi will confirm it."

Later that morning, Ixchel found herself walking alongside her parents through the narrow paths of their village, leading toward the small temple where Ah Kin Chi resided. Her heart pounded in her chest, a mix of dread and anticipation building with every step.

The priest was an old man, revered in their village for his knowledge of the gods and his connection to the spiritual world. He had lived through many seasons, his wisdom sought after by all who feared the divine. His home was simple, but the temple where he worked was adorned with symbols of the gods—jaguar masks, serpent carvings, and offerings of maize and cacao.

When they arrived, Ah Kin Chi greeted them with a calm smile, his eyes like dark pools of water, as if he could see straight through to

Ixchel's soul. He motioned for them to sit around the fire in the center of the temple's courtyard, the smell of burning incense filling the air.

"Ixchel," the priest began, his voice low and steady, "I hear you've had another vision."

She nodded, her throat tight. Her mother gave her a reassuring squeeze of the hand, encouraging her to speak. Slowly, Ixchel recounted the vision she had at the ceremony, describing the jaguar god, the flames, and the destruction of Yax Mutal. The words felt heavy as they left her lips, but she couldn't stop herself. It was as if telling Ah Kin Chi was her only hope of understanding what was happening to her.

The priest listened in silence, his face impassive. When she finished, he closed his eyes for a moment, his fingers tracing the lines of a carved jaguar amulet around his neck.

"Visions such as these are rare," he said finally, his voice slow and thoughtful. "The jaguar is a powerful symbol, both of protection and destruction. The fact that it appeared to you in flames... this is no small thing."

He opened his eyes and fixed his gaze on Ixchel. "The gods speak to us in many ways, child. Sometimes they send their messages through dreams, visions... but these messages are not always clear. What you saw may be a warning. Or it may be a test."

"A test?" Ixchel repeated, her brow furrowing. "What do you mean?"

Ah Kin Chi leaned forward slightly, his gaze never leaving hers. "The gods do not give gifts without a price. You may have the sight, but it does not mean that what you see is absolute. The future is always in motion, shifting with every decision we make. Your visions are a window into what could be, but they are not set in stone."

"But the city—Yax Mutal—it was burning," Ixchel said, her voice trembling. "How can I stop that?"

THE DAWN OF THE JAGUAR

The priest shook his head. "It is not always your place to stop it. Sometimes, the vision is merely meant to prepare you, to show you what is to come. The jaguar god you saw... it is both a protector and a destroyer. It may be that Yax Mutal's fate is tied to this god, and your role is not to prevent the flames, but to understand them."

Ixchel swallowed hard, fear tightening her chest. "And if the flames come? If the city is destroyed?"

"Then you will have a choice to make," Ah Kin Chi said gravely. "The gods give, and the gods take. But they do not always act in ways that we understand."

Her father, who had been silent until now, finally spoke up. "So, you believe her visions, then? You think she's been chosen?"

The priest's dark eyes flicked to Ahau, his expression unreadable. "It is not for me to say whether she has been chosen or cursed. That will be revealed in time. But one thing is certain—your daughter has been touched by the gods. And that is not a gift to take lightly."

A heavy silence fell over the group. Ixchel's mother clasped her hands tightly, her face pale with a mixture of awe and fear. Her father, though still skeptical, said nothing more. He could see the gravity in the priest's words, the weight of what his daughter might carry.

Finally, Ah Kin Chi rose from his seat, his robes rustling as he moved toward Ixchel. He placed a hand on her shoulder, his touch warm and surprisingly gentle for a man of his age.

"Whatever comes, Ixchel, you must be strong," he said softly. "The path before you

is not an easy one. But the gods have given you a gift. Whether it is a blessing or a curse... only time will tell."

As they left the temple, Ixchel felt the weight of the priest's words settle heavily on her shoulders. The flames, the jaguar, the destruction of Yax Mutal... it all loomed before her like a dark cloud. She didn't know what the gods wanted from her, or why they had chosen her to see these terrible things.

ANUPAM ROY

But one thing was clear—there was no turning back now.

Chapter 3: The Jaguar's Warning

The air was thick with the smell of burning incense and the sounds of celebration as Balam and his warriors entered the gates of Yax Mutal. The sun hung low in the sky, casting long shadows over the grand stone buildings and pyramids of the city. The people cheered, throwing flowers and shouting their praise as Balam rode through the streets, his expression calm but distant. His return was supposed to be a triumphant one. The campaign against the rival city-state had been a victory, another win for the kingdom of Yax Mutal.

Yet, as Balam looked out over the crowds, he could feel no joy.

He had returned, but something dark lingered in his heart.

His older brother, *Yaxuun*, stood waiting for him at the steps of the palace, clad in his ceremonial armor, his arms crossed over his broad chest. Yaxuun was every bit the warrior prince—strong, proud, and eager for battle. He was the king's favorite, the son destined to take the throne, and he wore that destiny like a crown.

Balam, on the other hand, had never felt at ease in his brother's shadow. He was not built for war the way Yaxuun was. He had always been quieter, more thoughtful, with a deep connection to the land and the people who lived on it. Battle was a necessity, not something to be glorified. Yet, it was his duty to serve his father and his city, so he fought when he had to.

As he dismounted, Yaxuun's smirk widened. "Little brother," he greeted, his tone mocking but familiar. "Back from another glorious victory, I see."

Balam met his brother's gaze, his face neutral. "It was a hard-fought battle. Many men lost their lives."

Yaxuun waved a hand dismissively. "Losses are expected. What matters is that the city remains strong. Father will be pleased."

"He cares more about the people than the victories," Balam said, his voice cool but controlled. "Or at least, he should."

Yaxuun's smile faded slightly, but before he could respond, the sound of footsteps echoed behind them. Their father, King *Jasaw Chan K'awiil I*, descended the palace steps, his regal robes trailing behind him, flanked by priests and advisors. His presence commanded respect, his eyes sharp with the weight of leadership. Though he was older now, there was still a strength about him, a determination in his stride that spoke of the great king he had been in his youth.

"Balam," the king greeted, his voice deep and filled with pride. "You have returned victorious once more. The gods smile upon us."

Balam bowed his head respectfully. "The gods were kind, Father. But the enemy grows stronger with each passing season."

The king nodded solemnly, his eyes narrowing slightly. "Yes, I have heard the reports. The city-states are restless. There is talk of alliances being formed against us. We must remain vigilant."

Yaxuun stepped forward, his chest puffed out. "We should strike first, Father. Crush them before they have the chance to unite. Yax Mutal has always been the strongest, and we must remind them of that."

Balam's jaw tightened. "There is more to strength than warfare, Yaxuun. The people grow weary of constant fighting. The land suffers. We cannot sustain endless war."

Yaxuun rolled his eyes. "Not this again. You and your endless concern for the commoners. The land will heal, as it always does. The people will endure. They serve us, not the other way around."

"The people are the city," Balam countered, his voice calm but firm. "Without them, we are nothing."

Before the argument could escalate, the king raised a hand, silencing both of his sons. "Enough," he said quietly. "There is wisdom in both of your words. But we must not act rashly. For now, we celebrate the victory that has been won. We will discuss the future in council."

Yaxuun nodded curtly, though it was clear he was not satisfied. He turned on his heel and strode away, leaving Balam standing beside their father.

The king placed a hand on Balam's shoulder, his eyes softening slightly. "You are troubled," he observed. "I can see it in your eyes."

Balam hesitated for a moment, unsure of how to explain the weight that had been pressing down on him since his return. "I've... been having dreams," he admitted quietly.

"Dreams?" The king's brow furrowed. "What kind of dreams?"

Balam glanced around, ensuring they were alone before he spoke again. "It's always the same. A jaguar, but not an ordinary one. It's enormous, with eyes that burn like fire. It watches me, and then it speaks. It says the city is doomed. That Yax Mutal will fall."

The king's face remained unreadable, though a flicker of concern passed through his eyes. "You've had this dream more than once?"

"Three times now," Balam said, his voice low. "Each time, the jaguar is closer. I can feel its breath on my skin. It tells me that the gods are displeased, that something terrible is coming."

King Jasaw Chan K'awiil I was silent for a long moment, his eyes studying his youngest son. Finally, he spoke, his voice measured. "The jaguar is a powerful symbol. It is both a protector and a harbinger of change. Dreams like these should not be ignored."

Balam looked at his father, surprised by his seriousness. "Do you think it's a warning?"

"I don't know," the king admitted. "But the gods speak to us in many ways, and they often choose those who are most connected to the spirit world to deliver their messages. You are not like your brother, Balam. You see things others cannot."

Balam felt a chill run down his spine. "So, what should I do?"

The king looked out over the city, his face grave. "We must consult the priests. The gods have been silent for too long, and this city has been through much. There may be a message in your dream that we have not yet understood."

Later that evening, as the celebrations wound down and the city settled into the quiet of night, Balam stood alone on one of the palace terraces, gazing out over the vast jungle that surrounded Yax Mutal. The stars glittered overhead, and the sounds of the night—crickets, distant howls of animals—filled the air. Yet, despite the beauty of the scene, he could not shake the feeling of unease that had taken root in his heart.

The dream had haunted him since the first night he had seen the jaguar. At first, he had dismissed it as nothing more than the result of exhaustion from the campaign. But after the second dream, he had started to wonder if there was something more to it. Now, after the third, he could no longer deny that the jaguar was trying to tell him something.

But what? And why him?

"Balam."

He turned to see his mother, *Lady K'awiil*, approaching. She was draped in a simple, elegant gown, her face soft with the wisdom of many years. There was always a calmness about her, a sense of inner peace that Balam had admired since he was a boy.

"You seem troubled," she said gently, coming to stand beside him.

Balam sighed, running a hand through his hair. "It's the dreams, Mother. The jaguar... it feels so real. And every time, it's the same message. The city is doomed."

Lady K'awiil's eyes darkened with concern, but she placed a comforting hand on his arm. "The jaguar is a sacred animal, beloved by the gods. It often appears in times of great change. Perhaps the gods are trying to tell you something."

THE DAWN OF THE JAGUAR

"I don't know if it's a warning or a threat," Balam said quietly. "But I fear for the city. Yaxuun wants to go to war again. Father listens to him, but I... I'm not so sure that's the path we should take."

His mother nodded thoughtfully. "Your father is a wise man, but Yaxuun... he has the heart of a warrior. He craves battle, and he believes that strength lies in conquest. But you, Balam, you understand that strength comes in many forms."

Balam turned to look at his mother, his eyes filled with uncertainty. "But what if I'm wrong? What if the jaguar is telling me that war is the only way to save the city?"

Lady K'awiil smiled softly. "The gods do not always speak plainly, my son. But they have given you a gift—the ability to see beyond the surface. Trust your instincts, and do not let fear guide your decisions. The path will reveal itself in time."

Balam looked back out over the city, the weight of responsibility settling heavily on his shoulders. The jaguar's fiery eyes still lingered in his mind, and the words it had spoken echoed in his ears.

The city is doomed.

But was it a warning? Or a challenge?

As the stars glittered above and the jungle whispered below, Balam could only hope that the gods would reveal their intentions soon—before it was too late.

own ambitions would guide him, as they always had.

Yuknoom turned and walked toward the wide stone balcony that overlooked the vast city of Calakmul. From this height, he could see the temples, the plazas, and the sprawling houses that stretched out into the dense jungle beyond. Calakmul had been a powerful kingdom for generations, and under his rule, it had become even more formidable. But Yax Mutal remained the one rival that refused to bow. The thought of conquering Yax Mutal had driven many of his decisions over the years, and now, it seemed that victory was finally within reach.

He closed his eyes, inhaling the humid jungle air, and considered the delicate balance of power that was now at play. Yaxuun's desire for war would be his undoing, and Balam's search for peace would leave him vulnerable. It was a rare opportunity, one that Yuknoom would not waste.

But the visions of the jaguar troubled him.

In the ancient stories of his people, the jaguar was not merely a symbol of power—it was the spirit that watched over kings, guided warriors, and sometimes delivered warnings from the gods. A jaguar appearing in visions, especially with such a grim message, could not be dismissed lightly. But Yuknoom was not a man to be swayed by fear. He was a king who made his own destiny.

Still, he knew he would need to tread carefully. The gods' favor could shift at any moment, and while he controlled men, no one truly controlled the will of the divine.

A soft footstep behind him broke his thoughts, and he turned to see his most trusted advisor, *Hunab*, a wise man who had served Calakmul for many years. He moved with the quiet dignity of one who had spent his life close to power.

"Sire," Hunab said, bowing slightly. "I have heard whispers from the temples. The priests speak of these visions as well."

Yuknoom nodded, motioning for Hunab to step closer. "The priests are always quick to interpret signs. What do they say?"

THE DAWN OF THE JAGUAR

Hunab hesitated before speaking, a rare show of uncertainty. "Some believe that the gods are warning of a great change—one that could affect both Yax Mutal and Calakmul. They speak of balance, of the jaguar as a guardian of the natural order. They fear that if the balance is disrupted, both cities could suffer."

Yuknoom's jaw clenched slightly. "The priests are superstitious. I care little for their warnings. What I need is certainty."

Hunab met the king's gaze, his expression calm but firm. "Even so, my lord, it would be wise to proceed with caution. The gods are watching, and sometimes their hand is felt more strongly in the affairs of men than we realize."

Yuknoom's eyes narrowed. "You sound like a priest yourself, Hunab."

The advisor did not flinch. "I am your servant, sire. And it is my duty to advise you wisely. The signs are there, whether we choose to heed them or not."

For a moment, Yuknoom was silent, his mind weighing the possibilities. He had never been one to ignore advice, especially when it came from someone as perceptive as Hunab. But he also knew that fear could be a dangerous motivator. If he allowed himself to be swayed by these visions, he risked losing the advantage he had worked so hard to gain.

"The gods may be watching," Yuknoom said finally, his voice measured. "But they do not rule this kingdom. I do. And I will see Yax Mutal fall."

Hunab bowed his head, accepting his king's decision. "As you command, my lord. The forces will be ready when the time comes."

Yuknoom turned back to the view of his city, his expression hardening. The jaguar might be a warning, but it was also a challenge. And if the gods were testing him, then he would prove to them, and to all of Mesoamerica, that he was the rightful ruler of the land.

"Send word to Iktan," Yuknoom said quietly. "Tell him to continue his work. The moment Yaxuun makes his move, we strike. Let the brothers tear each other apart."

Hunab nodded and slipped silently back into the shadows, leaving Yuknoom alone with his thoughts once more.

The jungle stretched out before him, dark and vast, hiding both enemies and allies within its depths. Somewhere, out there, the jaguar lurked, watching and waiting. Whether it was a guardian or an omen, Yuknoom did not know. But he would face it as he faced all challenges—without fear, and with a heart set on victory.

As the night deepened, Yuknoom's mind sharpened with focus. Yax Mutal's days were numbered. Whether it was by the hand of gods or men, the city would fall. And when it did, the name *Yuknoom Ch'een II* would be remembered as the king who finally conquered Yax Mutal.

In the silence of the night, the only sound was the distant, haunting call of a jaguar, echoing through the darkened jungle.

Chapter 4: Shadows in the Court of Yax Mutal

The air in Yax Mutal was thick with tension, an unease that lingered behind the walls of the great city. Though the sun hung high in the sky, casting the magnificent pyramids and stone palaces in a golden light, darkness brewed in the hearts of its people. The court of King Jasaw Chan K'awiil I bustled with nobles and courtiers, but beneath the pomp and ceremony, whispers of betrayal slithered like snakes.

In the neighboring kingdom of Calakmul, King Yuknoom Ch'een II watched from afar, his eyes fixed on Yax Mutal. Seated in his grand chamber, surrounded by advisors and warriors, Yuknoom grinned, his mind working through the intricate threads of war and politics. He had heard the rumors—Yax Mutal was not as unified as it appeared. There was discord between the king's sons, whispers of unrest among the nobles, and dissatisfaction among the people. Yuknoom intended to seize this opportunity.

He turned to one of his most trusted generals, a man named Ahaw Sak, who had long served him in the shadows. "It is time," Yuknoom said, his voice low and deliberate. "Send our spies into Yax Mutal. We must stoke the fires of division, weaken them from within."

Ahaw Sak, clad in the traditional garb of a warrior, nodded. "It shall be done, my lord. The seeds of discord have already been planted. Now we must water them."

Yuknoom leaned back on his throne, his fingers drumming on the armrest. "Soon, Yax Mutal will fall, not by brute force, but by its own hand."

At the palace in Yax Mutal, tension simmered. Balam walked through the palace gardens, his mind troubled. Though his father's rule was strong, Balam sensed the fractures within the kingdom. His brother Yaxuun was growing restless, his ambition dangerous. In the court, factions were forming, each whispering of a different future for Yax Mutal. And the looming threat of Calakmul was ever-present, like a storm waiting on the horizon.

Balam entered the chamber where his father, King Jasaw Chan K'awiil I, was seated on his throne, his advisors gathered around him. The air was thick with the scent of incense, and the walls were adorned with vibrant murals of past victories.

"Father," Balam began, bowing respectfully. "I have heard troubling news from the borderlands. Calakmul has been unusually quiet."

The king, a man of stern presence and wise eyes, looked up at his son. "Calakmul is always quiet before they strike," he replied, his voice heavy with experience. "Yuknoom Ch'een II is cunning. He seeks to divide us, to weaken us before his armies march."

Balam nodded, his face grave. "I fear the divisions are already here, father. Yaxuun grows restless, and there are whispers of dissent among the nobles. We must be vigilant."

The king's gaze hardened, his eyes narrowing as he considered his son's words. "Yaxuun has always been ambitious, but I will not tolerate treachery in my own court. As for the nobles, they forget their place. I will remind them."

One of the advisors, an old man with a long, braided beard, stepped forward. "My lord," he began cautiously, "there are rumors that Calakmul has already sent spies into our city. It is said they walk among us, listening, observing."

Jasaw Chan K'awiil's expression darkened. "Spies? In my city?" He clenched his fist, the muscles in his jaw tightening. "We will root them out. We will find whoever has betrayed Yax Mutal and make an example of them."

Balam stepped closer to his father. "We must tread carefully, father. If we act too quickly, we risk driving our own people further into fear and rebellion. Calakmul seeks to divide us—if we turn on our own too soon, they will succeed without lifting a sword."

The king considered his son's words. "You are wise, Balam," he said, though his voice still carried the weight of frustration. "But we cannot afford to be passive. We must show strength, or Calakmul will see it as weakness."

"Strength, yes," Balam agreed. "But we must also be cunning. We need to control the narrative in our court before Calakmul's lies take root. I suggest we send our own spies to Calakmul. Learn what they are planning."

The old advisor nodded in agreement. "A wise strategy, my king. We must strike in the shadows as well as on the battlefield."

King Jasaw Chan K'awiil leaned back in his throne, his brow furrowed in thought. "Very well," he said at last. "Balam, you will oversee this. Send word to our most trusted men. We will learn what Calakmul intends."

Balam bowed again. "It will be done."

As Balam left the throne room, he felt the weight of responsibility settle heavily on his shoulders. His father was a great king, but the kingdom was fragile. He knew Yaxuun's ambition would only grow, and Calakmul would take every opportunity to exploit the kingdom's weaknesses.

In the shadows of the palace, the whispers grew louder. The nobles spoke in hushed tones, their loyalty no longer as certain as it once was. And in the streets, the people of Yax Mutal began to feel the chill of uncertainty. They looked to the heavens for signs, but the gods remained silent.

Far from the palace, in a darkened room in the heart of Yax Mutal, a man sat hunched over a table, carefully reading a message etched into a thin strip of bark paper. He was a spy—one of Calakmul's eyes within Yax Mutal. He had come as a merchant, selling pottery and textiles in the city's market. But his true purpose was far more dangerous.

The message was from Calakmul, from Ahaw Sak himself. It contained instructions, a new phase in the plan to weaken Yax Mutal. The spy's eyes flickered over the words, a smile creeping onto his lips. Soon, the city would turn on itself. Soon, the great Yax Mutal would fall.

He burned the message and disappeared into the night, his mission clear.

Back in the court of Calakmul, Yuknoom Ch'een II sat on his throne, gazing out over the horizon. His spies were in place. The seeds of chaos had been planted. Now, it was only a matter of time before Yax Mutal would crumble from within.

"Soon," he whispered to himself, "very soon, the great city of Yax Mutal will bow before me."

His generals and advisors stood at attention, waiting for his command. But Yuknoom knew that this war would not be won with swords alone. It would be won in the shadows, with whispers and secrets.

And as the shadows grew longer in Yax Mutal, the fate of the city—and of its people—hung in the balance.

Chapter 5: The Flames of Fate

The evening sky was painted in brilliant hues of red and gold as the sun dipped below the horizon, casting long shadows over Ixchel's village. The day had been calm, like many others, with her father tending the fields and her mother preparing the evening meal. Ixchel had spent her time near the forest, gathering herbs for her mother. Life in the village had always been simple, and though the weight of her visions sometimes haunted her, she found comfort in the familiar rhythm of her home.

But the peace would not last.

It began with a distant rumble, like the rolling of thunder. Ixchel paused, her basket of herbs clutched in her hands, and turned her gaze toward the edge of the village. The sound grew louder—hooves pounding against the earth, accompanied by shouts. Her heart clenched in her chest as she realized what was happening.

Bandits.

She dropped the basket and ran toward her home as fast as her legs would carry her, the sounds of chaos growing louder with each step. Flames flickered in the distance, and soon she could see the figures of armed men on horseback, their faces hidden beneath masks, their swords gleaming in the fading light. Her breath caught in her throat. They weren't just bandits—they carried the banners of *Calakmul*.

Her village was under attack.

"Ixchel!" her mother's voice rang out, frantic and trembling with fear.

She found her mother standing at the doorway of their home, her face pale, her hands trembling as she clutched a small bundle of belongings. "We must leave, quickly!"

"Where's Father?" Ixchel asked, panic rising in her chest as she glanced around, searching for her father's familiar figure.

Her mother shook her head, her eyes filled with grief. "He went to defend the village... he told us to run."

A sickening dread filled Ixchel's stomach. Her father was a strong man, but he was no warrior. He was a farmer, like most of the men in the village. They were no match for trained soldiers from Calakmul. But there was no time to think—no time to mourn. The bandits were closing in, and the flames were spreading.

"Come," her mother urged, pulling Ixchel by the arm. "We must go!"

They fled into the night, along with the other villagers who had managed to escape the initial wave of violence. The jungle loomed ahead, dark and forbidding, but it was their only chance. Behind them, the screams of those left behind echoed in the air, mingling with the crackling of the flames. Ixchel's heart ached with every step, but she pushed forward, driven by the need to survive.

As they ran, Ixchel's thoughts swirled in confusion and fear. Why would Calakmul send raiders to their small, insignificant village? What could they possibly want here? But deep down, she knew the answer. Calakmul was at war with Yax Mutal, and her village was caught in the middle of the conflict. The bandits were likely mercenaries, hired to disrupt and terrorize the lands allied with Yax Mutal.

Suddenly, a sharp cry pierced the air behind them.

"Ixchel, run!" her mother screamed as one of the masked raiders spotted them.

He charged toward them, a cruel smile visible beneath his mask. Ixchel froze for a moment, terror gripping her, but her mother shoved her forward.

"Go! I'll hold him off!"

"No!" Ixchel screamed, trying to pull her mother along with her, but it was too late.

THE DAWN OF THE JAGUAR

The raider was upon them. He grabbed her mother by the arm, tearing her away from Ixchel, and threw her to the ground. Ixchel watched in horror as the man raised his sword, but before he could strike, a loud crash interrupted the scene—a tree branch, heavy and rotted, fell between the raider and her mother, sending him stumbling back.

It was enough. Ixchel grabbed her mother's hand and pulled her to her feet. They ran, their bodies moving on instinct as they disappeared into the jungle, the sounds of the raider's curses fading behind them.

For what felt like hours, they ran, not stopping until they were deep within the trees, where the air was thick with the smell of damp earth and leaves. Only then did they collapse to the ground, their bodies trembling with exhaustion.

"I can't... I can't run anymore," her mother gasped, clutching her chest. Her face was pale, her breath coming in ragged bursts.

Ixchel knelt beside her, tears streaming down her face. "We have to keep moving, Mama. We can't stop."

But her mother shook her head, her eyes filled with sorrow. "Go, Ixchel. You must reach Yax Mutal. Find refuge there."

"I'm not leaving you," Ixchel said, her voice choked with emotion. "We'll go together."

Before her mother could protest, something stirred within Ixchel. A familiar sensation—the same feeling she had when her visions came. Her breath caught as the world around her began to shift. The jungle darkened, the sounds of the night fading away, replaced by an eerie stillness.

And then, she saw it.

The jaguar.

It appeared in front of her, its golden eyes gleaming in the shadows. The massive creature stared at her, unblinking, as if it had been waiting for this moment. Ixchel's heart pounded in her chest, but she couldn't look away. The jaguar's presence filled the air with an almost tangible power, and for a moment, time seemed to stand still.

The jaguar stepped forward, its gaze locking onto hers. And then, without a sound, it turned and began to walk deeper into the jungle.

Ixchel knew what it meant. The jaguar was showing her the way. A hidden path—one that would lead them to safety. She had no choice but to follow.

"Mama," she whispered, turning to her mother. "I know where we need to go."

Her mother looked at her, confused and weary, but she nodded. "Lead the way, Ixchel."

They followed the jaguar through the thick underbrush, their feet moving as if guided by an unseen force. The jungle seemed to part for them, the path becoming clearer with each step. It was as if the jaguar was clearing the way, leading them toward a destination only it knew.

Hours passed, and just when Ixchel thought they could go no further, the trees began to thin. In the distance, she saw the towering silhouette of a city rising above the jungle canopy.

Yax Mutal.

"We made it," Ixchel breathed, relief washing over her.

Her mother collapsed beside her, too exhausted to speak. They had survived. They had escaped the bandits, and now they stood on the edge of the great city, where they could find refuge.

But even as they approached the gates, Ixchel's mind was filled with the image of the jaguar. It had saved them, led them to safety. But why? What was the jaguar trying to tell her?

As they entered the city, she couldn't shake the feeling that the jaguar's presence was more than just a symbol of protection. It was a warning. A reminder that the gods were watching, and that her journey was far from over.

And deep within the shadows of Yax Mutal, where the grand temples loomed and the priests whispered of omens, Ixchel knew that her visions would only grow stronger. The jaguar had more to show her. And whatever lay ahead, it was tied to the fate of both her and the city she now called home.

That night, as Ixchel and her mother found shelter among the refugees in the outskirts of Yax Mutal, Ixchel's dreams were filled with fire and shadow. The jaguar appeared again, this time leading her through the winding streets of the city, past temples and palaces, toward a hidden place—a secret path that only she could see.

When she woke, drenched in sweat, the jaguar's eyes still burned in her mind.

There was a hidden path within Yax Mutal.

And the jaguar wanted her to find it.

Chapter 6: The Meeting of Fate

The grand city of Yax Mutal stood like a sentinel amidst the jungle, its towering temples and sprawling palaces a symbol of its power and resilience. For Balam, the youngest son of King Jasaw Chan K'awiil I, the city had always been both a sanctuary and a burden. His life, though draped in privilege, was shadowed by expectations he had little desire to fulfill. Unlike his older brother Yaxuun, Balam was not driven by conquest or power. He sought something deeper—a connection to the gods, an understanding of the visions that plagued his dreams.

And now, standing at the gates of the city, watching the refugees pour in from the surrounding villages, he felt that something was changing. Among the sea of faces, there was one that stood out—a girl, not much younger than himself, with dark, determined eyes that seemed to hold a secret she had yet to reveal.

Balam's gaze lingered on her as she and her family approached, weary from their journey. He noticed how she held herself differently from the others, her head high despite the exhaustion etched on her face. There was something about her presence that stirred the same feeling he had experienced in his dreams—an echo of the jaguar that haunted him.

"Who is she?" he asked one of his guards, his voice low.

The guard glanced in the direction of the girl, then back at Balam. "A refugee, my lord. Her village was raided by bandits from Calakmul."

Balam nodded, though his curiosity was far from satisfied. He could not shake the sense that their fates were intertwined. He stepped forward, moving through the crowd of refugees until he stood before the girl and her family.

"You," Balam said, his voice gentle but commanding, "what is your name?"

The girl looked up, startled by the attention, her eyes meeting his with a mixture of surprise and caution. She glanced at her mother, who was too tired to protest, and then back at Balam.

"Ixchel," she said softly. "I am from the village of Xul."

Balam studied her for a moment, his gaze unwavering. "And you fled because of the raids?"

Ixchel nodded, but there was something in her eyes that told him there was more to the story. He could feel it in the air, an unspoken connection between them that neither could yet explain.

"I have heard rumors," Balam continued, his voice lowering so only she could hear, "that you have been touched by the gods."

Ixchel's breath caught in her throat. How could he know? How could this prince, someone so far removed from her world, sense what she had kept hidden from so many?

"I... I don't know what you mean," she stammered, though her heart raced with the fear that he might know more than she realized.

Balam tilted his head slightly, his dark eyes narrowing as if trying to peer into her soul. "I think you do. The jaguar... it has come to you, hasn't it?"

Ixchel's eyes widened in shock. She hadn't told anyone about her visions, not since leaving the village. And yet here, this stranger—this prince—knew about the jaguar.

"How do you know that?" she whispered, her voice trembling.

Balam's expression softened. "Because it has come to me as well. In my dreams. The jaguar speaks of doom, of fire, of something that threatens Yax Mutal. I believe the gods are trying to warn us... but I do not yet understand why."

Ixchel swallowed hard, the weight of her visions suddenly feeling much heavier. She had always thought her connection to the jaguar god was her burden alone to carry, but now she realized she was not alone. And if the prince had been having the same visions, then perhaps it wasn't just a warning for her—but for the entire city.

THE DAWN OF THE JAGUAR

"I saw the jaguar again, on the night we fled," she said quietly, her voice barely more than a whisper. "It showed me the way to Yax Mutal... but I think it wants me to do more."

Balam nodded, his suspicions confirmed. This girl was not just a refugee. She was part of something larger, something that he had been struggling to understand for months.

"You must come with me to the palace," Balam said, the decision made in his mind. "The high priests must hear of this. They will know what to do."

Ixchel's mother, who had been standing nearby, suddenly stepped forward, her face pale with fear. "No, my lord, please! My daughter is just a girl. She is not meant for the palace."

Balam turned to her, his expression calm but resolute. "Your daughter is chosen by the gods, whether you believe it or not. If her visions are true, then she holds the key to protecting Yax Mutal."

Ixchel's mother looked at him, her lips trembling as she tried to speak. She wanted to protest, to keep her daughter safe, but deep down she knew that Ixchel had been different from the others since she was a child. The gods had indeed touched her, and there was no escaping that truth.

"Let her go," her mother whispered finally, her voice breaking with emotion. "If this is her fate, then let it be so."

Ixchel glanced at her mother, a mixture of relief and sadness washing over her. She didn't want to leave her family, not after everything they had been through. But there was something deep inside her that told her Balam was right. She had been chosen for a reason, and whatever lay ahead, she had to face it.

"I will go," Ixchel said quietly, turning back to Balam. "But what if your brother disagrees? I have heard he is not fond of outsiders."

Balam's jaw tightened at the mention of his brother, Yaxuun. It was true—Yaxuun was quick to dismiss anyone who did not serve his immediate interests, and he had little patience for what he considered "superstitions." But Balam was not afraid of his brother's disapproval.

"Leave Yaxuun to me," Balam said firmly. "What matters now is what the gods have shown us. Come."

With a nod, Ixchel followed Balam through the streets of Yax Mutal, her heart pounding with a mixture of fear and anticipation. The city's grandeur overwhelmed her senses—the towering temples, the bustling markets, the distant chants of priests performing their sacred rituals. It was all so different from the simple life she had known.

As they approached the palace gates, Balam glanced at her. "Are you afraid?"

Ixchel hesitated before answering. "Yes. But not of what lies within the palace."

Balam smiled faintly, understanding her meaning. "Good. Fear of the unknown is natural, but we must not let it control us."

They passed through the grand stone gates and entered the palace grounds, where the air was thick with incense and the sounds of chanting priests. The high priests, Balam knew, would be performing their evening rites in the inner sanctum, where the great temple of the jaguar god loomed.

Balam led Ixchel to a quiet chamber near the temple, where they were greeted by one of the senior priests, Ah Kin Chi. His white robes flowed around him like mist, and his eyes, sharp and perceptive, immediately focused on Ixchel.

"Prince Balam," Ah Kin Chi said in a low, reverent tone, bowing slightly. "You bring a visitor."

"This is Ixchel," Balam explained, his voice steady. "She has had visions of the jaguar god. The same visions I have seen. I believe she is connected to whatever is coming."

Ah Kin Chi's eyes narrowed as he studied Ixchel. "The jaguar has come to many in these troubled times... but not all are chosen."

"I am not asking for your permission," Balam said, his tone taking on a firmer edge. "I am asking for your guidance. If the gods have sent her, we must know why."

The priest considered this for a moment, then nodded. "Very well. Let her speak."

Ixchel took a deep breath and stepped forward, her voice steady but laced with uncertainty. "The jaguar showed me a hidden path, a way through the city. I believe it is meant for something greater, but I don't know what."

Ah Kin Chi's expression softened slightly, as if he had expected as much. "The gods speak in riddles, child. But the jaguar is a guardian. If it is showing you a path, then it is one that leads to either salvation or destruction."

Balam exchanged a glance with Ixchel, both of them sensing the gravity of the moment.

"Then we must be prepared," Balam said quietly. "For whatever the gods intend."

Ah Kin Chi nodded solemnly. "Yes, Prince. We must. But be warned—what the gods give, they can also take away."

Ixchel felt a chill run down her spine at the priest's words. The path ahead was uncertain, but there was no turning back now. She had been chosen, and whatever the jaguar god had in store for her and for Yax Mutal, she would face it.

Together, with Balam at her side.

Chapter 7: Shadows of Doubt

Yax Mutal was a city of immense grandeur, but beneath its towering temples and sacred courtyards, shadows of intrigue and distrust lurked. The elite, those who advised the king and governed the city alongside the royal family, thrived on whispers and suspicion. And with the arrival of a mysterious girl from the outskirts of the kingdom, the atmosphere had grown thick with fear and rumors.

Ixchel had only been in the palace for two days, but already, her presence had sparked unease. The nobility watched her with wary eyes, and the servants spoke in hushed tones whenever she passed. She could feel the weight of their judgment with every step she took. Even though she had barely seen Balam since he brought her to the palace, the gravity of his trust in her had not lessened the uncertainty she felt.

In the grand hall of the palace, Balam stood before a gathering of the city's elite, his dark eyes resolute as he spoke on Ixchel's behalf.

"She is not a threat," he said firmly, his voice carrying through the chamber. "The gods have sent her to us with visions that could save Yax Mutal. We must listen."

But his older brother, Yaxuun, seated at the head of the table with the other advisors, was less than convinced. His sharp features twisted into a sneer, his arms crossed over his chest. "A girl from a peasant village," Yaxuun said, his voice dripping with disdain. "And you believe she has been chosen by the gods? Balam, you are a fool to trust her so blindly."

Balam's fists clenched at his sides, his patience wearing thin. "I am not blind, brother. The jaguar god has appeared in my dreams as well. Ixchel's visions align with what I have seen. There is a connection between us—between her and the fate of Yax Mutal."

Yaxuun laughed, a cold, mocking sound that echoed in the hall. "Your dreams are nothing but the fantasies of a young man who spends too much time in the temples. The girl could be a spy for Calakmul, sent to deceive us while they prepare to strike."

Murmurs of agreement rippled through the assembled nobles, and Balam felt the sting of their doubt. But he held his ground. "Calakmul would not send someone like her—she is a simple girl, not a warrior or diplomat. And if she were a spy, why would she speak so openly of her visions? The gods are speaking through her, whether you choose to believe it or not."

Yaxuun stood from his seat, towering over Balam. His eyes glinted with malice, the rivalry between the brothers simmering just beneath the surface. "You speak of gods and visions, but all I see is a city in danger. Calakmul is our enemy, and we cannot afford to take chances. This girl is a threat to our security, and I will not allow her to stay within these walls."

Before Balam could respond, one of the advisors, a man named Chacal, stood and addressed the court. "My lords, we cannot ignore the possibility that the girl may be an agent of Calakmul. There have been whispers in the city... rumors that she brings ill omens. If the people believe she is a danger, it could incite unrest."

Balam's heart sank as the tide of opinion turned against him. He could see the fear in the eyes of the nobles, the way they clung to their suspicions. Ixchel had come to the city as a refugee, but now she was seen as a symbol of chaos.

"We must act swiftly," Yaxuun declared, his voice ringing with authority. "The girl will be imprisoned until we can determine the truth of her intentions."

Balam stepped forward, his voice rising with urgency. "You cannot do this! Imprisoning her will only drive us further from the gods' will. If you lock her away, you risk angering the very forces we need to guide us."

THE DAWN OF THE JAGUAR

Yaxuun's eyes flashed with anger. "I am responsible for the safety of this city, not you, Balam. And I will do what is necessary to protect it."

Before Balam could protest further, two guards entered the hall at Yaxuun's command. They moved toward Ixchel, who stood at the far end of the room, her expression unreadable. She had remained silent throughout the debate, knowing that anything she said would only fuel the accusations against her.

The guards grabbed her roughly by the arms, and though Ixchel did not resist, her eyes flickered with a deep, quiet fear.

"Take her to the dungeons," Yaxuun ordered, his tone final. "She will remain there until I am satisfied that she poses no threat."

Balam felt a surge of helplessness as he watched Ixchel being led away, her figure disappearing into the shadows of the palace corridors. He knew that once she was imprisoned, it would be nearly impossible to free her. The city's elite, already on edge, would use her as a scapegoat for their own fears.

Later that night, Balam found himself pacing the halls outside the chambers of the high priests. He had tried to appeal to them, to convince them that Ixchel's visions were a sign from the gods, but they had been reluctant to intervene. Their loyalty to the throne—and to Yaxuun—was too strong.

"Balam," a familiar voice called softly from the shadows.

He turned to see Ah Kin Chi, the senior priest who had been present when Ixchel first spoke of her visions. The old man's face was lined with worry, his hands folded into his robes as he approached.

"I have heard what has happened," Ah Kin Chi said, his voice filled with regret. "The court is divided, and the people fear what they do not understand."

Balam stopped pacing and faced the priest, desperation in his eyes. "They're going to keep her in the dungeons, Ah Kin Chi. She's done nothing wrong, but Yaxuun and the nobles won't listen. They see her as a threat."

Ah Kin Chi nodded slowly. "It is not uncommon for those touched by the gods to be feared, even by those who claim to serve them. But you must be careful, Balam. Your brother's jealousy runs deep, and if you challenge him too openly, it may put you in danger as well."

Balam's jaw clenched. "I don't care about the danger. Ixchel's visions are real, and they may be the only thing that can save this city. I have to do something."

Ah Kin Chi sighed, his gaze softening. "Then you must find another way to prove her innocence. The court will not listen to words alone. There must be a sign—a message from the gods that cannot be denied."

Balam stared at the priest, his mind racing. "A sign… but what kind of sign?"

Ah Kin Chi's eyes gleamed with a knowing light. "You have seen the jaguar in your dreams, just as she has. If the jaguar god truly speaks to both of you, then it will guide you. But the path will not be easy."

Balam nodded, determination hardening within him. He would find a way to free Ixchel, no matter what it took.

Down in the dark, damp dungeons beneath the palace, Ixchel sat alone in a small, cold cell. The stone walls seemed to press in on her, and the air was thick with the smell of mildew and decay. She had never imagined herself in such a place—surrounded by criminals, treated like a traitor to the very city she had sought to protect.

But even here, in the suffocating darkness, the presence of the jaguar god lingered.

She closed her eyes, trying to focus, to feel the familiar pulse of the jaguar's energy. It was faint, like a distant whisper, but it was there. The jaguar had not abandoned her.

As she sat in the stillness, her thoughts returned to Balam. He had believed in her when no one else would, even when his own brother had turned against him. She couldn't let him down. She couldn't let Yax Mutal fall.

THE DAWN OF THE JAGUAR

The jaguar's image flickered in her mind, and with it, a sense of purpose began to take shape. There was something she had yet to understand—something hidden within the city that could change everything.

And as the night wore on, Ixchel vowed to find it.

Whatever the jaguar god had in store for her, she would be ready.

In the days that followed, Balam searched relentlessly for a way to prove Ixchel's innocence. He spoke to the high priests, consulted ancient texts, and even ventured into the jungle in search of answers. But the city's tension only grew, and Yaxuun's grip on power tightened.

Rumors of Calakmul's spies infiltrating Yax Mutal spread like wildfire, and with each passing day, more people began to turn against Ixchel. The nobles, once uncertain, were now convinced that the girl was an omen of disaster.

But Balam refused to give up.

And in the darkest hour, just as hope seemed to be slipping away, the jaguar came to him once again.

This time, it did not speak of doom.

It spoke of a hidden truth buried deep within the heart of Yax Mutal—a truth that only Ixchel could uncover.

Chapter 8: The Flight into the Jungle

The night was heavy with the hum of the jungle as Balam paced the length of his chamber, the walls closing in around him with each passing moment. The weight of the city's judgment pressed hard on his shoulders, the doubt of the nobles, and most of all, Yaxuun's unrelenting grip on power. Ixchel, the one person who could help him understand the visions of the jaguar god, was locked away in the dungeons, and time was slipping away.

Balam knew he had to act—before it was too late. But how could he free her from the depths of the palace without alerting Yaxuun's ever-watchful guards?

A knock at the door broke his frantic thoughts, and when it opened, a familiar figure shuffled inside—Ah Kin Chi, the old priest whose wisdom had been a constant source of guidance for him.

"My lord," the priest began, his voice low and urgent, "I have come with news that cannot wait."

Balam's brow furrowed. "What is it? Is it about Ixchel?"

Ah Kin Chi nodded gravely, his eyes filled with an intensity that sent a chill through Balam's spine. "Yes, but it is more than that. I have had my own visions, Balam, and they confirm what we feared. The jaguar god, Balam, the protector of our city... he is preparing to pass judgment on Yax Mutal."

Balam's heart raced. "Judgment? What do you mean?"

"The gods are not blind to the corruption within our walls," Ah Kin Chi continued, his voice growing more urgent. "Yaxuun's ambition, the nobles' greed, the people's descent into fear and mistrust—all of it has angered the gods. If we do not act, the jaguar will bring destruction to our city."

Balam stared at the priest, the enormity of his words sinking in. "Then what must we do? How do we stop this?"

"There is a way," Ah Kin Chi said, his voice barely a whisper now, as if the very walls were listening. "You and Ixchel must leave Yax Mutal—tonight. There is a sacred pilgrimage you must undertake, to the Cenote of Itzamná, where the gods can be reached directly. Only there can you commune with them and plead for the city's salvation."

Balam's mind raced. The Cenote of Itzamná was a distant, sacred place, far into the jungle, where few had ever ventured. It was said to be a gateway between the mortal world and the gods, where priests and kings had once gone to receive divine guidance. But the journey would be perilous, and time was not on their side.

"And Ixchel?" Balam asked. "How do I free her from the dungeons?"

Ah Kin Chi's eyes gleamed with a knowing light. "I have made arrangements. There is a hidden passage beneath the temple of the jaguar, an old tunnel that leads out of the city. I will help you both escape, but we must move quickly."

Balam felt a surge of hope, a spark of possibility in the midst of the darkness that had consumed him. If there was even a chance that they could prevent the jaguar god's wrath, he had to take it.

"Then let's not waste any more time," Balam said, his voice steady with resolve. "Lead me to her."

The palace dungeons were damp and suffocating, the air thick with the scent of decay. The guards at the entrance, familiar with Ah Kin Chi's presence as a high priest, paid little attention as he and Balam descended into the depths. Their footsteps echoed through the narrow stone corridor, each step bringing them closer to Ixchel's cell.

When they reached the door, Ah Kin Chi produced a small key from his robes and unlocked the heavy iron gate. The door creaked open, revealing Ixchel huddled in the corner, her face pale but her eyes still burning with quiet determination.

THE DAWN OF THE JAGUAR

"Ixchel," Balam said softly, stepping into the cell. "We don't have much time. We're getting you out of here."

Ixchel stood slowly, her eyes meeting Balam's. There was a moment of silence between them, an unspoken understanding passing through the air. She had always known her fate was tied to something larger, and now, it was becoming clear.

"How?" she asked, her voice steady but laced with curiosity.

Ah Kin Chi stepped forward. "There is a hidden passage beneath the temple of the jaguar. It will lead you out of the city and into the jungle. From there, you must journey to the Cenote of Itzamná."

"The Cenote..." Ixchel whispered, her eyes widening. She had heard stories of the sacred place, where the gods could be reached, but she had never imagined she would be called to such a task. "The gods... they want us to go there?"

"Yes," Ah Kin Chi said gravely. "The jaguar god is preparing to pass judgment on Yax Mutal. But if you reach the cenote and commune with the gods, there may still be a chance to save the city."

Balam reached for her hand, a silent reassurance that they would face this together. "We can't stay here any longer. Yaxuun will stop at nothing to see you imprisoned—or worse. We must leave now."

Ixchel nodded, her heart pounding with both fear and anticipation. "I'm ready."

The passage beneath the temple of the jaguar was dark and narrow, the walls damp and slick with moss. Balam and Ixchel moved quickly, with Ah Kin Chi leading the way through the twisting tunnel. The air was thick and cool, and the only sound was the quiet drip of water from the stones above.

As they emerged into the dense jungle outside the city, the moonlight filtered through the canopy, casting eerie shadows on the ground. The jungle seemed alive with the rustling of leaves and the distant calls of nocturnal creatures. But for Balam and Ixchel, there was no time to admire the beauty of the night. The journey ahead was long, and the weight of their mission hung heavy in the air.

Ah Kin Chi stopped at the edge of the trees, his old eyes gleaming with wisdom as he turned to face them. "The path to the Cenote of Itzamná is not easy. You will face many challenges, both from the jungle and from within yourselves. But the gods are with you."

Balam clasped the priest's arm in gratitude. "Thank you, Ah Kin Chi. For everything."

The priest smiled, his face softening. "I have faith in you both. The gods do not choose lightly, and they have chosen you for a reason."

Ixchel, her heart still racing from the escape, looked up at the sky, where the stars glittered faintly through the trees. "How will we know the way to the cenote?"

"The jaguar will guide you," Ah Kin Chi said simply, his gaze turning to Ixchel. "Trust in the visions. The jaguar god is watching over you."

With that, the old priest turned and disappeared into the shadows of the jungle, leaving Balam and Ixchel alone with the vast wilderness before them.

For a moment, they stood in silence, the enormity of what they were about to undertake settling over them like a cloak. The jungle was both beautiful and dangerous, and the cenote, their only hope, lay somewhere deep within its heart.

"We have to keep moving," Balam said, his voice quiet but firm. "We can't stay near the city for too long. Yaxuun will send scouts to look for us."

Ixchel nodded, her thoughts still swirling with the weight of her visions. "I know. But the jaguar god... it feels closer now. Like it's leading us."

Balam glanced at her, his gaze softening. "I trust you, Ixchel. Whatever happens, we will face it together."

THE DAWN OF THE JAGUAR

The words, though simple, filled Ixchel with a sense of comfort she hadn't felt since her father's death. In Balam, she had found someone who understood the weight of her burden, someone who shared in the mystery of the jaguar's warnings.

With a determined nod, they set off into the jungle, the dense foliage closing in around them as they made their way deeper into the unknown. The path ahead was uncertain, but they knew one thing for sure: the fate of Yax Mutal rested in their hands.

And as the distant roar of the jaguar echoed through the night, Ixchel felt the stirrings of the divine, guiding her every step.

The journey to the Cenote of Itzamná had begun.

Chapter 9: Trials of the Jungle

The jungle was alive. Every step Balam and Ixchel took through the dense underbrush felt as though the forest itself was watching them, its eyes hidden in the leaves, its whispers carried on the wind. The humid air clung to their skin, and the tangled roots and vines beneath their feet slowed their progress. But they pressed on, driven by the urgency of their mission and the weight of the prophecy that hung between them.

The Cenote of Itzamná lay far ahead, deep in the heart of the jungle. And with each passing hour, the dangers around them became more palpable.

Ixchel, her breath coming in shallow bursts, glanced at Balam as they trudged forward. His face was a mask of concentration, his hand always close to the hilt of his obsidian blade, ready for whatever threats the jungle might unleash. Though he was a warrior, strong and sure, there was a softness in his gaze when he looked at her—a shared understanding of the burden they both carried.

"We need to find higher ground before nightfall," Balam said, his voice breaking through the sound of the forest. "The predators here are more dangerous in the dark."

Ixchel nodded, wiping the sweat from her brow. She could feel the energy of the jaguar god pulsing faintly in the back of her mind, a constant reminder that their journey was not just physical but spiritual. Yet the weight of it all was exhausting.

"Do you think we're close to the cenote?" she asked, her voice barely above a whisper, as if afraid the jungle itself might answer.

Balam shook his head. "Not yet. But we'll know when we are." He paused, his gaze searching the horizon. "The jaguar... it will guide us."

They walked in silence for a while, their senses heightened, attuned to every rustle and chirp. But as the shadows of the trees lengthened and the golden light of the sun dimmed, the jungle seemed to shift, its atmosphere growing heavier, more oppressive.

Suddenly, Balam stopped in his tracks, his body tensing.

"Ixchel," he whispered, his hand reaching out to stop her. "Stay close."

She didn't need to ask why. The look in his eyes told her everything she needed to know—danger was near.

From the thicket ahead, there was a faint rustling, followed by the unmistakable sound of voices. They were faint at first, but as Balam and Ixchel crouched low, moving behind a large tree trunk, the voices grew clearer, laced with tension.

"Mayan warriors," Balam murmured under his breath, his eyes narrowing. "They're not from Yax Mutal."

Ixchel's heart raced as she peered through the leaves. Ahead of them, a small band of warriors—five, maybe six—moved stealthily through the jungle, their faces painted with the markings of a rival city. They carried spears and shields, their movements purposeful, as if they were searching for something—or someone.

"Do you think they're from Calakmul?" Ixchel asked, her voice tight with fear.

"Most likely," Balam replied, his grip tightening on his weapon. "They may have been sent to track us."

Panic welled in Ixchel's chest, but Balam's presence beside her was a calming force. She glanced at him, taking in his steady posture, the way his eyes never wavered from the threat ahead.

"We need to avoid them," Balam whispered. "There's no need for a fight, not unless we're forced to."

Ixchel nodded, her heart pounding in her ears. Together, they moved silently through the underbrush, careful to stay out of sight.

THE DAWN OF THE JAGUAR

Every step felt like a gamble, each rustle of leaves sending a jolt of anxiety through her veins.

But then, just as they were about to pass the group unnoticed, one of the warriors halted abruptly. He sniffed the air, his head turning in their direction.

Balam's grip on Ixchel's arm tightened. "Don't move," he mouthed.

The warrior's eyes narrowed, scanning the area. For a moment, time seemed to stretch endlessly, the tension unbearable. Then, with a sharp signal to his comrades, the warrior began moving toward them, his spear raised, suspicion etched on his face.

Balam's body tensed, ready to spring into action.

"Run," he whispered urgently to Ixchel.

She hesitated, her heart pounding. "But—"

"Run!"

Without another word, Ixchel bolted, darting through the thick jungle foliage. Behind her, she could hear the sounds of a struggle—Balam's grunts as he clashed with the warriors, the sharp clang of obsidian against stone.

She didn't want to leave him. Every instinct screamed to turn back, but she knew she couldn't help him by staying. So she ran, her feet pounding against the earth, the sounds of the jungle blurring around her.

After what felt like an eternity, the jungle opened up, and she found herself at the edge of a riverbank. Gasping for breath, Ixchel collapsed to her knees, her chest heaving. The water glistened in the fading light, but it brought her no comfort.

"Balam..." she whispered, fear twisting in her gut.

Moments later, the underbrush rustled behind her, and she whipped around, her heart in her throat.

Balam emerged, bruised and bloodied, but alive. Relief flooded her chest as she rushed to him.

"You're hurt!" she exclaimed, her hands reaching for the cuts along his arm and shoulder.

"It's nothing," Balam said, wincing as he wiped blood from his brow. "We don't have time to stop. They'll be looking for us."

"But—"

"Ixchel," he said firmly, his eyes locking with hers. "We have to keep moving. The jaguar god is testing us, and this is just the beginning."

She swallowed hard, nodding. He was right. The jungle wasn't going to make their journey easy. This was just one of many trials they would face.

As they moved along the riverbank, the light continued to fade, and the sounds of the jungle grew louder—the calls of birds, the rustling of leaves, and the distant howls of creatures that neither of them wished to meet.

It wasn't long before the darkness fully enveloped them. Balam led the way, his senses attuned to the jungle's rhythms, but Ixchel could feel something else in the air—something beyond the natural dangers that surrounded them.

A cold wind swept through the trees, and Ixchel shivered, though the night was warm. She slowed her pace, glancing around nervously.

"Balam," she whispered, her voice barely audible. "Something's watching us."

Balam halted, his eyes scanning the shadows. "What do you mean?"

"I don't know," Ixchel admitted, her voice trembling. "It feels... unnatural."

Balam's gaze hardened. "Stay close."

As they continued forward, the strange presence lingered, growing more oppressive with each step. The trees seemed to twist unnaturally, their branches curling toward them like claws. And then, without warning, a deep, guttural growl echoed through the forest.

THE DAWN OF THE JAGUAR

Ixchel froze, her heart leaping into her throat. The growl wasn't from any animal she knew. It was something else—something ancient, something tied to the very land they walked on.

Balam drew his blade, his muscles tense as he scanned the trees. "Ixchel, get behind me."

Suddenly, the growl came again, louder this time, closer. From the shadows, a pair of glowing eyes appeared, followed by the sleek, muscular form of a jaguar—its fur dark as the night, its eyes glowing with an eerie, unnatural light.

But this wasn't just any jaguar. Ixchel could feel it in her bones. This was a manifestation of the jaguar god itself—a warning, or perhaps a challenge.

The jaguar stalked toward them, its movements slow and deliberate, its eyes never leaving Ixchel. She could feel its gaze boring into her, as if it was searching her soul, testing her resolve.

"What do we do?" she whispered, her voice trembling.

Balam stood his ground, his blade raised. "We don't run."

The jaguar growled again, a low, rumbling sound that seemed to vibrate through the ground beneath their feet. But then, just as suddenly as it had appeared, the jaguar stopped, its eyes locking with Ixchel's.

For a moment, the world seemed to stand still. And then, with a graceful turn, the jaguar disappeared back into the shadows, leaving them alone once more.

Balam exhaled slowly, lowering his blade. "It's testing us. The jaguar god... it's watching."

Ixchel nodded, her heart still racing. "We passed... for now."

As the night wore on, they continued their journey, their bond deepening with each shared danger, each trial. The jungle, with all its threats and mysteries, was forcing them to confront not just the dangers around them, but their own fears and doubts.

And though the path ahead was uncertain, one thing was clear: they were in this together. Balam and Ixchel, bound by prophecy, by fate, and by the jaguar god's watchful gaze.

They would face whatever came next—together.

Chapter 10: Shadows in the Palace

The palace of Yax Mutal was bathed in the soft light of the setting sun, casting long shadows across its ancient stone corridors. As the evening descended, so too did a quiet tension over the city. While the people of Yax Mutal busied themselves with their evening rituals, the palace harbored a more insidious atmosphere—one of ambition, jealousy, and betrayal.

Yaxuun, the eldest son of King Jasaw Chan K'awiil I, stood at the edge of the palace balcony, his hands gripping the cold stone rail as he gazed out over the sprawling city below. The sky was a brilliant blend of red and gold, yet to Yaxuun, it felt more like the dying embers of a fire he had yet to stoke. His heart was restless, his mind whirling with thoughts that had darkened in the shadows of his father's reign.

"All of this will be mine one day," he whispered to himself, his voice low and harsh. "But not soon enough."

Behind him, footsteps echoed softly, and Yaxuun didn't need to turn to know who it was. His most trusted advisor and ally, Itzam, approached him with the quiet grace of a serpent. Itzam, a man of middling stature but sharp intellect, had served Yaxuun in secret for years, feeding his ambitions with subtle words and dangerous ideas.

"It is as you feared," Itzam said quietly as he stopped beside Yaxuun. "The city grows uneasy. The people speak of visions, omens... whispers that the gods are displeased."

Yaxuun's jaw tightened. "Ixchel," he muttered, venom dripping from the name. "That peasant girl has poisoned the minds of our people. And now Balam—he sees her as some sort of prophet."

Itzam's eyes gleamed with intrigue. "Balam is becoming a problem, my lord. His sympathy for the girl and the growing fascination with the gods could undermine your position. The people look to him as the king's favored son."

Yaxuun's face twisted into a sneer. His younger brother, Balam, had always been a thorn in his side. Though Yaxuun was the eldest and the rightful heir, Balam's wisdom, tempered by his lack of bloodlust, had made him popular among the people and, more importantly, among the priests. While Yaxuun sought power through strength and conquest, Balam found favor through diplomacy and understanding—a quality Yaxuun loathed.

"He is weak," Yaxuun spat. "Father indulges him, but it is I who have fought, I who have shed blood for Yax Mutal. And yet, Balam grows closer to the throne every day."

Itzam gave a small, calculating nod. "That is why you must act now, my lord. The people speak of war with Calakmul as inevitable, and the gods' omens only fan the flames. But you can turn this unrest to your advantage."

Yaxuun turned, his dark eyes gleaming with anticipation. "Go on."

Itzam smiled, his thin lips curling. "Calakmul's king, Yuknoom Ch'een II, has sent emissaries to our court in secret. They are eager to weaken Yax Mutal, to see it crumble from within. You could offer them what they desire."

Yaxuun's brow furrowed. "An alliance with Calakmul?" His voice was hesitant for a moment, though the temptation of power quickly smothered any doubts. "Father would never agree to such treachery."

"It does not matter what your father agrees to," Itzam said smoothly, his tone chilling. "It is *you* who will rule Yax Mutal, and if you secure an alliance with Calakmul now, your ascent to the throne will be swift and uncontested."

Yaxuun turned back to the city, the weight of Itzam's words settling heavily on his shoulders. He had always considered Calakmul the enemy, a rival city whose influence threatened Yax Mutal's dominance in the region. But now, as the fires of his ambition burned brighter, he saw the potential in what Itzam suggested. An alliance with Calakmul, if done in secret, could strengthen his position and help him remove the final obstacle to his power—his father.

"And what of Balam?" Yaxuun asked, his voice sharp. "He will oppose me. The people will rally to him."

Itzam's eyes flickered with amusement. "Leave Balam to me, my lord. There are ways to turn even the most beloved of men into enemies of the state. He will not be a threat for long."

Yaxuun's lips curled into a grim smile. It was a dangerous plan, but danger had never deterred him before. He was a warrior, a conqueror, and now, more than ever, he was ready to conquer Yax Mutal itself.

"Send word to Calakmul," Yaxuun said, his voice low but firm. "Tell them I am open to negotiations."

Itzam bowed deeply, the smile never leaving his face. "As you command, my lord. The future of Yax Mutal will soon be in your hands."

As Itzam slipped silently into the shadows, Yaxuun remained on the balcony, staring down at the city that would one day be his. But his thoughts were not of peace or prosperity. They were of power, of dominance, and of the day when his father's reign would end.

Later that night, Yaxuun met with a small group of trusted soldiers in a hidden chamber beneath the palace. These men were loyal to him alone, bound by promises of wealth and status once he claimed the throne. Among them was K'awiil, a seasoned warrior whose loyalty to Yaxuun stemmed from years of fighting by his side.

"My lord," K'awiil said, kneeling before Yaxuun, "we have heard rumors of unrest among the people. Some say they fear the gods' wrath, others whisper of war with Calakmul. What are your orders?"

Yaxuun regarded K'awiil for a moment before speaking. "The people must not fear the gods, nor should they think of Balam as their savior. We will plant seeds of doubt, turn their fear into anger—against my brother, against my father. They will see that the true strength of Yax Mutal lies in me."

K'awiil nodded, his expression hard. "And the priests, my lord? They are loyal to the king and Balam."

Yaxuun's eyes darkened. "The priests will be dealt with in time. But for now, we focus on Calakmul. I will speak with their emissaries and ensure that we have their support when the time comes."

Another soldier stepped forward, a young man named Chak, who had recently sworn his allegiance to Yaxuun. His voice trembled slightly as he spoke. "And if King Jasaw Chan K'awiil learns of our plans?"

Yaxuun's smile was cold. "He won't. Not until it is too late."

Meanwhile, in the royal chambers, King Jasaw Chan K'awiil I sat in deep contemplation, unaware of the plots forming against him. His thoughts were heavy with the weight of the kingdom's future. The omens troubled him, and the growing tensions with Calakmul were like a storm on the horizon, one he could no longer ignore.

But his greatest concern was his sons.

Balam, his youngest, had always been a source of pride. His wisdom, compassion, and connection to the spiritual realm had made him beloved among the people. But Yaxuun... Yaxuun was a different matter. Though a fierce warrior, his ambition often clouded his judgment, and the king feared that ambition would one day drive him to rash decisions.

"Father," a voice interrupted his thoughts.

Jasaw looked up to see Balam entering the room, his face etched with concern.

"Balam," the king said, motioning for him to sit. "What troubles you, my son?"

"I fear for Yax Mutal," Balam replied, his voice steady but filled with worry. "The visions... they speak of danger, of a reckoning. And there are whispers of unrest among the people. I believe we must take action, but not through war."

The king studied his son, nodding slowly. "You speak wisely, Balam. But war may be inevitable. Calakmul will not rest until they see us fall."

Balam shook his head. "There is another way, Father. If we can unite the people, strengthen our connection to the gods—"

Before he could finish, Yaxuun entered the room, his expression unreadable.

"Father, brother," Yaxuun said, his voice smooth. "I have come to discuss the growing threat of Calakmul. We must act, and we must act soon."

The king's eyes flickered between his two sons, sensing the tension between them. He knew that Yaxuun was driven by ambition, but Balam's vision of peace was clear.

"War may come," Jasaw said gravely, "but it will not be without cost."

Yaxuun's lips thinned as he bowed his head slightly, hiding the calculations racing through his mind. Soon, he thought. Soon, the throne would be his.

And Yax Mutal would bow to him—or burn.

Chapter 11: The Battle at the Sacred Cenote

The jungle loomed heavy with the weight of ancient secrets as Balam and Ixchel pressed onward, their footsteps muted by the dense undergrowth. The air around them was thick with humidity, the sounds of wildlife echoing like a distant, haunting chorus. Despite the perilous journey, they had finally reached the edge of the Sacred Cenote of Itzamná, the place where they would seek the gods' wisdom. The great sinkhole yawned before them, its dark waters shimmering in the faint light that filtered through the trees.

"This is it," Balam whispered, his voice tight with awe and exhaustion. His dark eyes scanned the surroundings, and despite the beauty of the place, he couldn't shake a sense of unease. "The gods' resting place."

Ixchel stood beside him, her eyes wide, both in reverence and fear. The visions of the jaguar god had drawn her here, but now that they stood at the edge of the cenote, an overwhelming dread settled over her.

"Do you feel it?" Ixchel asked, clutching her cloak tightly around her. "The power of this place—it's as though the very earth hums with the gods' voices."

Balam nodded, but his thoughts were elsewhere. The jungle had been unkind to them—wild beasts, treacherous terrain, and enemy warriors had tested their resolve at every turn. Yet, they had survived. But now, something darker stirred in the shadows of the trees.

"I don't like this," Balam said, his hand resting on the hilt of his sword. "We're being watched."

Ixchel stiffened at his words, her instincts sharpening. The journey had taught her to trust Balam's warrior senses, and now, as she peered into the thick foliage surrounding them, she too felt it—a presence lurking, hidden but near.

"Who would follow us here?" Ixchel asked, her voice barely above a whisper.

As if in answer, a rustling sound erupted from the trees. From the shadows emerged a group of men, their eyes burning with malevolent intent. They wore the distinctive garb of priests, but their faces were painted with warlike symbols, their expressions cruel. Leading them was a tall man with piercing eyes and an aura of authority—Ahaw Sak, one of Calakmul's most ambitious priests. His face was twisted in a smile that sent a chill through Ixchel's spine.

"You've traveled far," Ahaw Sak called out mockingly, stepping forward with slow, deliberate steps. "But your journey ends here."

Balam instinctively placed himself between Ixchel and the approaching priests, his grip tightening on his sword. "Who are you?" he demanded, though he already knew the answer.

"Ahaw Sak," the man said, his smile widening. "Priest of Calakmul and guardian of the old ways. You are trespassing on sacred ground, prince."

"Sacred ground?" Balam's voice was steady, though his heart pounded in his chest. "We have come to seek the gods' wisdom, to prevent the destruction of Yax Mutal. Why would you stand in our way?"

Ahaw Sak chuckled, the sound harsh and cold. "Yax Mutal's fate is sealed, young prince. The gods have no more favor for your city. Calakmul's rise is inevitable. And those who seek to preserve Yax Mutal stand in defiance of the divine order."

Ixchel, her voice trembling with anger, stepped forward. "The jaguar god speaks to us! He calls for balance, not destruction. You cannot claim to serve the gods while sowing chaos."

THE DAWN OF THE JAGUAR

Ahaw Sak's smile faltered, but his eyes remained fixed on Ixchel. "You are nothing more than a girl who plays with powers she cannot understand. The gods will not listen to the likes of you."

In a blur of movement, Ahaw Sak raised his hand, and the priests behind him sprang into action. Balam barely had time to draw his sword before the first of the rogue priests was upon him. Steel clashed against steel as Balam fought to hold his ground, his skill as a warrior tested to its limits.

"Stay behind me!" Balam shouted to Ixchel, though she was already moving, grabbing a fallen branch to defend herself.

The jungle exploded into chaos. The rogue priests, though fewer in number, were relentless, their strikes precise and deadly. Balam parried a blow aimed at his head, then spun to slash at another attacker's side. He moved with the grace and power of a seasoned warrior, but there were too many of them, and Ahaw Sak stood back, watching the battle unfold with cold calculation.

"Fools," Ahaw Sak hissed, his eyes narrowing as he observed Balam's skill. "You cannot defy fate."

Balam gritted his teeth, his muscles screaming with exhaustion as he fended off another strike. Sweat dripped down his brow, his heart racing. He could feel the weight of the battle pressing down on him, the odds stacked against them. But he couldn't give up. Not now.

"Balam!" Ixchel's voice rang out, sharp with urgency. She had managed to fend off one of the priests, but another was closing in on her, his dagger gleaming in the dim light.

Without hesitation, Balam lunged toward her, knocking the priest to the ground with a powerful blow. But in that moment of distraction, he left himself open. He barely registered the flash of movement before the pain hit—a searing, white-hot agony in his side. A blade had found its mark.

He staggered, his vision swimming as he felt the blood pouring from the wound. The jungle seemed to tilt around him, the sounds of the battle growing distant.

"Balam!" Ixchel screamed, rushing to his side as he fell to his knees, his sword slipping from his grasp.

Ahaw Sak stepped forward, his eyes gleaming with triumph. "It seems the gods have spoken after all," he said, his voice dripping with malice. "Yax Mutal will fall, and you... you will die here, prince."

Ixchel knelt beside Balam, her hands shaking as she pressed them against his wound, trying to stem the bleeding. "No," she whispered, her voice breaking. "This can't be how it ends."

Balam's breath came in ragged gasps, his vision blurring as he looked up at Ixchel. "It's... not over," he rasped, his voice barely audible. "We... must reach the cenote."

Ahaw Sak raised his hand, signaling his remaining priests to close in. But before they could advance, a deep rumble echoed through the jungle—a sound that seemed to come from the very earth itself. The rogue priests hesitated, looking around in confusion.

"What... what is that?" one of them muttered, his voice trembling.

Ahaw Sak frowned, his confident demeanor faltering as the rumbling grew louder. The ground beneath their feet began to shake, and from the dark waters of the cenote, a low, growling sound emerged—a sound that sent a chill down everyone's spine.

"The jaguar god," Ixchel whispered, her eyes wide with realization. "He's here."

A deafening roar erupted from the cenote, and from the depths of the dark waters, a massive, shadowy figure began to rise. It was the jaguar god, its eyes glowing with an otherworldly light, its powerful form emerging like a nightmare from the abyss.

The rogue priests froze in terror, their weapons falling from their hands as the god's presence filled the air, overwhelming and undeniable.

THE DAWN OF THE JAGUAR

Ahaw Sak took a step back, his face pale. "No... this cannot be," he muttered, his voice shaking.

But it was too late. The jaguar god roared once more, and with a wave of its massive paw, the rogue priests were thrown back, their bodies crashing against the trees with a force that left them broken and motionless.

Ahaw Sak, his eyes wide with fear, turned to run, but the jaguar god's gaze fell upon him, and in an instant, he was gone—swallowed by the shadows of the jungle.

Ixchel, trembling with shock and awe, turned to Balam. He was barely conscious, his breath shallow, but he was alive.

"We made it," she whispered, tears filling her eyes as she cradled his head in her lap. "We made it, Balam."

The jaguar god's glowing eyes met hers, and for a moment, time seemed to stand still. Then, slowly, the god retreated back into the cenote, its form dissolving into the waters until it was gone.

The jungle fell silent.

Ixchel looked down at Balam, her heart pounding with fear and hope. "Hold on," she whispered. "We still have a long way to go."

Chapter 12: Into the Waters of Destiny

The jungle surrounded the Cenote of Itzamná, its dense foliage trembling with an unseen energy. The wind whistled through the towering trees, and the waters below shimmered like liquid obsidian under the moon's gaze. Ixchel stood at the edge of the sacred cenote, her heart pounding in her chest. The moment had come—the visions had led her here, and now she had to face what awaited in the depths below.

Balam stood by her side, his hand resting on the hilt of his blade, his eyes scanning the horizon for any sign of danger. Despite his own wounds and fatigue from their journey, his focus was solely on Ixchel. He could see the tension in her frame, the weight of the prophecy pressing down on her slender shoulders.

"Are you certain?" Balam asked, his voice low but steady. "Once you enter those waters, there is no turning back."

Ixchel nodded, though her gaze remained fixed on the still surface of the cenote. "I have no choice, Balam. The gods... they have called me. I must know what they intend for Yax Mutal."

Balam clenched his jaw, his concern for her palpable. "Then I will wait here. I will guard you, as always."

She turned to him, her hand brushing his. "I know you will, but this journey, I must take alone."

The two of them shared a look, one filled with the silent understanding that had grown between them. Their bond had deepened over the course of their journey—more than simply comrades, more than allies bound by destiny. They were intertwined by forces far greater than either of them could comprehend. And yet, the weight of that bond, along with the burden of prophecy, sat heavily between them.

Taking a deep breath, Ixchel stepped closer to the edge of the cenote, her bare feet brushing the cool stone. She could feel the pull of the waters, the ancient power that radiated from beneath the surface. Without another word, she took the plunge, her body diving gracefully into the depths.

The water enveloped her, cold and suffocating for a moment before it became something else entirely—warm, almost comforting. She felt herself sinking deeper, farther than she had anticipated. Darkness surrounded her, but she didn't panic. She allowed herself to descend, knowing that the gods were waiting.

In the inky blackness of the cenote's depths, time seemed to lose all meaning. Ixchel's lungs should have been burning, her body straining for air, but she felt none of it. Instead, she felt weightless, as though suspended between worlds. The water swirled around her, and she was no longer alone.

A soft glow began to emanate from below, a faint light that gradually grew brighter. The water parted, and suddenly, Ixchel found herself standing on solid ground—not at the bottom of the cenote, but in an entirely different realm.

The world around her was otherworldly. The sky above was a deep violet, streaked with golden clouds, and the ground beneath her feet shimmered like polished stone. Strange, luminous plants and towering trees surrounded her, their leaves glowing with an ethereal light. In the distance, the great temples of the gods rose, majestic and timeless.

Before her stood three figures—divine and imposing, their forms flickering with energy. The tallest of the figures, draped in jaguar pelts and crowned with the feathers of a quetzal, stepped forward. His eyes, glowing like embers, fixed on her. He was Itzamná, the chief of the gods, and his presence filled Ixchel with awe.

Beside him stood Chaac, the god of rain and storms, his skin the color of the deepest clouds, his eyes crackling with lightning. On the

THE DAWN OF THE JAGUAR

other side was Ix Chel, the goddess of the moon and medicine, her form serene and bathed in a soft glow.

"It is time, child of Yax Mutal," Itzamná spoke, his voice echoing in the space between worlds. "The prophecy that has been whispered through the winds, etched in stone, and carried in your visions must be fulfilled."

Ixchel swallowed, her throat dry despite the strange waters she had emerged from. "You've shown me glimpses of the future—war, destruction. But what must be done to save Yax Mutal?"

The gods exchanged glances, a silent conversation passing between them. Finally, Ix Chel, her namesake, stepped forward. Her voice was soft, yet filled with a power that reverberated through the air. "The path ahead is one of blood and sacrifice. The war between Yax Mutal and Calakmul is not merely a conflict between cities, but a battle between the realms of the human and the divine."

Chaac's voice thundered like a storm. "Calakmul's ambition has not gone unnoticed by the gods. Their king seeks to dominate not only the lands of men but to challenge the gods themselves. His heart burns with arrogance, and he believes he can turn the will of the heavens."

Ixchel's heart raced. She had not imagined such a thing. "What must we do to stop him? Balam... and I—we will fight to protect our city, but how can we oppose forces that defy even the gods?"

Itzamná stepped forward once more, his eyes narrowing. "The final confrontation approaches. The human world and the divine world are intertwined in ways you do not yet understand. The jaguar, the protector of your city, must face the forces that seek to unseat him. But the price will be steep."

Ix Chel raised her hand, and Ixchel felt the warmth of the goddess's presence surround her. "You, Ixchel, are the key. Your visions have guided you to this moment, but your role is not yet fully revealed. The future of Yax Mutal lies not only in the strength of warriors but in the rituals that connect your people to the divine. There are ancient rites that must be completed to summon the full power of the jaguar god."

Ixchel's brow furrowed. "Rituals? What must I do?"

"It is not just you," Ix Chel continued. "Balam must face his destiny as well. He is tied to the jaguar in ways neither of you yet fully comprehend. But there is sacrifice in all things, and the gods do not intervene without a price."

At the mention of sacrifice, Ixchel felt a chill run down her spine. "What kind of sacrifice?"

The gods remained silent for a moment, their forms flickering like the flames of a distant fire. It was Chaac who finally spoke. "The royal bloodline of Yax Mutal is bound to the jaguar god. In order for the city to be saved, the bloodline must be broken."

Ixchel's heart sank. "Broken? What does that mean for Balam?"

Itzamná's eyes softened, though his expression remained somber. "That is not for us to reveal. But know this, Ixchel—when the time comes, you will understand. You must prepare for the trials ahead, for they will test not only your strength but your very soul."

The weight of their words pressed heavily upon her. She had come seeking answers, and though she had received them, they carried a terrible burden. She glanced up at the gods, their forms shimmering in the strange light.

"Thank you," Ixchel whispered, though her heart ached with the uncertainty of what lay ahead.

Ix Chel stepped forward, her eyes kind but filled with ancient knowledge. "Go now, child. Return to your world, for the path is set. Walk it with courage and wisdom."

With that, the realm around Ixchel began to fade, the brilliant light dimming until she was once again surrounded by the dark, cold waters of the cenote. Her body was pulled upwards, towards the surface, as if carried by unseen hands.

THE DAWN OF THE JAGUAR

She broke through the surface with a gasp, the air filling her lungs as she blinked against the starlight. The familiar jungle sounds returned, the rustling leaves, the distant calls of night creatures. Balam was there, pulling her from the water, his strong arms lifting her onto the stone edge of the cenote.

"Ixchel," he breathed, concern etched across his face. "What did you see?"

Ixchel looked into his eyes, the weight of the gods' words still heavy in her chest. "The gods have spoken. The future of Yax Mutal... and of us... is bound to a final battle. But Balam," her voice faltered, "the price will be greater than either of us could have imagined."

Balam held her gaze, his own eyes filled with resolve. "Whatever the cost, we will face it together."

As they stood on the edge of the cenote, the jungle around them quiet and still, the weight of destiny pressed down on their shoulders. The final confrontation was coming—between the cities, between the gods, and between the lives they had known and the future that awaited them.

Chapter 13: Return to a City on the Brink

The jungle echoed with the sound of rustling leaves and distant birdsong as Ixchel and Balam trudged through the dense foliage, the weight of their journey heavy upon them. They had been traveling for days, making their way back to Yax Mutal. Each step brought them closer to home, but also closer to the danger that now loomed over the city like a storm cloud ready to burst.

Balam's wounds, though still fresh, had miraculously begun to heal after his encounter with the jaguar god. The divine presence had bestowed upon him a strength he hadn't felt before. His skin, still marked with scars, glowed with an otherworldly resilience. It was as if the jaguar god had left a piece of himself within Balam, a mark of his favor.

"I never thought I would see Yax Mutal again," Balam murmured, his voice heavy with both relief and apprehension. "But what kind of city will we return to?"

Ixchel walked beside him, her brow furrowed with worry. "The gods have given us a mission, but Yaxuun... he's dangerous. He's always craved power, and now he sees his chance."

Balam clenched his jaw, his thoughts darkening at the mention of his brother. Yaxuun had always been ambitious, but Balam had never imagined he would betray their father, the great king Jasaw Chan K'awiil. The thought of his brother seizing the throne through deceit and treachery filled him with both anger and sorrow.

"If Yaxuun has made his move, the city may already be on the verge of war," Balam said grimly. "My father's rule has always been strong, but Yaxuun knows how to manipulate the elite. He'll twist their loyalty against him."

Ixchel nodded, her hand absentmindedly touching the stone the gods had given her. It was cool to the touch, a constant reminder of the task they had been given. "We must act quickly," she said softly. "Before it's too late."

As they reached the outskirts of Yax Mutal, the once-familiar landscape took on an ominous tone. The towering temples and sprawling city that usually stood as a symbol of power and unity now seemed shrouded in uncertainty. Smoke rose from distant fires, and the sounds of unrest echoed faintly in the air.

"The city is restless," Balam observed, his eyes narrowing as they approached the gates. "Something is happening."

Two guards stood watch at the entrance, their faces hard with tension. When they spotted Balam, their eyes widened in surprise. One of them stepped forward hesitantly, recognizing the prince.

"Prince Balam!" the guard exclaimed. "We thought... we thought you were dead. Word came that you were wounded during the campaign."

"I nearly was," Balam replied, his voice steady. "But I've returned. What is happening here?"

The guard hesitated, glancing at his companion before answering. "Yaxuun... your brother has declared himself heir to the throne. He claims your father is too weak to lead the city, and many of the noble families support him. The people are divided, and tensions are high. There are rumors of an uprising."

Balam's heart sank. His worst fears were confirmed. Yaxuun had moved swiftly in his absence, capitalizing on their father's vulnerabilities. "And my father?" he asked, his voice tight with concern.

"He remains in the palace, but... he's isolated. His loyalists are few, and Yaxuun has surrounded him with his own forces. The city is on the edge of civil war."

THE DAWN OF THE JAGUAR

Balam exchanged a glance with Ixchel. The gods had sent them back for a reason, but now they faced a city tearing itself apart from within.

"We must reach the palace," Balam said firmly. "My father needs to know the truth of what's happening, and we need to stop Yaxuun before this gets out of control."

The guard nodded and stepped aside to allow them passage. "Be careful, Prince Balam. Yaxuun has eyes everywhere."

As they made their way through the city streets, the tension was palpable. Groups of citizens whispered in huddles, casting furtive glances toward the palace. The markets, once bustling with life, were eerily quiet. Soldiers loyal to Yaxuun patrolled the streets, their presence a constant reminder of the power struggle brewing beneath the surface.

"They're scared," Ixchel whispered, her eyes scanning the faces of the people. "They don't know who to trust."

"And that's exactly what Yaxuun wants," Balam replied, his voice bitter. "If the people are divided, he can seize control more easily."

They arrived at the palace, its towering structure now more imposing than ever. Balam led Ixchel through a side entrance, avoiding the main gates where Yaxuun's guards were likely stationed. Inside, the atmosphere was tense, and the usually bustling halls were eerily quiet.

They made their way to the royal chambers, where Balam knew his father would be. As they approached the door, they were stopped by a familiar figure—Ah Kin Chi, the high priest. His face was grave, his eyes filled with worry.

"Balam," the priest whispered, his voice filled with relief. "You've returned."

"I have," Balam replied, his tone urgent. "Where is my father? We need to speak with him."

Ah Kin Chi sighed heavily. "The king... he is weak, Balam. His health has worsened since you left, and Yaxuun has used this to his advantage. He's turned many of the nobles against your father, and there are whispers that he will soon declare himself king."

"We cannot let that happen," Balam said, his voice filled with determination. "My father is still the rightful ruler of Yax Mutal."

"There's more," Ah Kin Chi continued, glancing nervously around. "Yaxuun has made contact with Calakmul. He seeks their support to solidify his claim to the throne. If he succeeds... the city will fall."

Ixchel's heart pounded in her chest. The vision she had seen—the jaguar god warning of the city's destruction—was coming to pass. "We need to act now," she said, her voice steady. "The gods have spoken. Yaxuun's betrayal is a threat not only to Yax Mutal but to the balance of the divine and human worlds."

Ah Kin Chi nodded solemnly. "The gods have shown us their displeasure. The city is in chaos, and if Yaxuun seizes power with the help of Calakmul, it will be the end of Yax Mutal as we know it."

Balam clenched his fists. "Then we stop him. We rally those who remain loyal to my father and take back the city."

Ah Kin Chi placed a hand on Balam's shoulder. "The people will follow you, Balam. You are the rightful heir, and they trust you. But you must move quickly, for Yaxuun will not hesitate."

Balam nodded, his resolve hardening. "We will stop him. I swear it."

As they prepared to confront Yaxuun, Ixchel felt the weight of her visions pressing upon her. The gods had brought her to this moment for a reason, and now it was time to fulfill her role in the prophecy. The fate of Yax Mutal hung in the balance, and the final confrontation was drawing near.

Balam, now standing taller than ever, met her gaze with fierce determination. "We fight for our city," he said quietly, his voice steady.

"And for the future of our people," Ixchel replied, gripping the stone gifted by the gods. The battle for Yax Mutal was just beginning, but together, they would face whatever came next.

Chapter 14: The Gathering Storm

The sky over Yax Mutal darkened as the city prepared for war. Heavy clouds hung low, casting a shadow over the sacred temples, the city's towering pyramids seeming less like symbols of strength and more like looming sentinels to an uncertain future. Inside the palace, King Jasaw Chan K'awiil I sat upon his throne, his once-mighty frame now weakened with age and illness, but his mind sharp as ever. He was surrounded by his most loyal advisors, generals, and priests, all of them tense with the knowledge that Calakmul's armies were on the march.

"The reports confirm it," Ah Kin Chi said, stepping forward. The high priest's voice carried the weight of the coming storm. "K'ahk' Tiliw Chan Chaak leads the army of Calakmul, and they are advancing toward Yax Mutal as we speak. They will arrive within days."

A murmur of unease spread through the chamber, but the king remained silent, his eyes fixed on a map laid out before him. The lines and symbols, representing cities, rivers, and battlegrounds, swirled in his mind like the pieces of a puzzle he had yet to solve.

"We are surrounded," General Ik'al declared, his tone laced with urgency. "Yaxuun's treachery from within, Calakmul's forces from without. The people will panic if they learn how dire the situation truly is."

"The people already feel it," Balam said, stepping forward. He had returned to the palace with Ixchel, and though his wounds had healed, the weight of responsibility pressed heavily upon him. His eyes burned with determination as he stood beside his father. "They know war is coming. They know we are at the edge of something far greater than a simple conflict."

The king finally spoke, his voice low and steady, though it crackled with age. "War is always far greater than a conflict, Balam. It is the reckoning of nations, the fate of kings and the lives of the innocent caught in its wake." He paused, his gaze shifting to the horizon. "But Calakmul has been waiting for this moment for generations. Their ambition knows no bounds. They will not rest until Yax Mutal falls."

Ixchel, standing silently at Balam's side, felt the air grow thick with tension. Her heart pounded as she recalled the vision that had brought her here, the jaguar god's warning of Yax Mutal's destruction. This was the moment the gods had foretold—the storm that would engulf the city if they did not act.

"Father," Balam said, his voice firm. "We must prepare the people. We must unite them. If Yaxuun is allowed to sow further division, we will be too weak to resist Calakmul's invasion."

The king's eyes turned to his youngest son, studying him for a long moment. Balam had always been different—thoughtful, reflective. Not a warrior by nature, like his brother Yaxuun. But now, in the face of all that threatened Yax Mutal, he saw something more in Balam. A strength that transcended the battlefield.

"You are right," the king finally said, his voice heavy with both weariness and resolve. "We must rally the people. Yaxuun's treachery has fractured the city, but we must make them see that their future lies in unity, not in division."

Ixchel stepped forward, her voice steady and clear. "The gods have spoken. They have shown me that the balance between the divine and mortal realms is tipping. If Yax Mutal falls, it will be more than just the loss of a city. It will be the end of an era, a break in the connection between the gods and the people."

The priests in the room exchanged uneasy glances, but Ah Kin Chi nodded, his eyes reflecting both belief and fear. "Ixchel speaks the truth. The omens have been clear, even if we wished to deny them. We must act quickly."

"What do you propose?" the king asked, leaning forward slightly on his throne.

THE DAWN OF THE JAGUAR

Balam stepped closer, his voice firm but respectful. "Father, let me lead the charge to rally the people. I will go to the heart of the city and speak to the citizens. They need to hear from someone they trust, someone who stands for unity and the future of Yax Mutal."

The king's eyes softened as he regarded his son. "And you think they will follow you?"

"I do," Balam replied, his voice unwavering. "But they need to know that we stand together. They need to see strength and resolve from their leaders, not the division that Yaxuun has planted."

Jasaw Chan K'awiil I sat back, considering his son's words. "And what of Yaxuun?" he asked, his voice cold. "If he learns of your plan, he will strike."

Balam clenched his fists, his jaw tightening. "Yaxuun has already made his move. But he cannot hold power without the people. If we can turn them against him, his support will crumble."

Ixchel felt the weight of the moment pressing upon them. She knew the gods had brought her and Balam together for this very reason. She stepped closer to the king, her voice soft but filled with conviction. "The jaguar god has marked Balam. He is meant to lead this city through the storm. But it will not be easy. Yaxuun will not give up without a fight."

The king's eyes flickered with a mixture of pride and sorrow as he looked at his son. "Then it is decided," he said quietly. "Balam, you will rally the people. But you must be careful. Yaxuun will not sit idly by as you move against him."

Balam nodded, a fire of determination burning in his chest. "I will not fail."

The king rose slowly from his throne, his frailty more evident than ever as he stood. He placed a hand on Balam's shoulder. "I know you won't, my son."

The room fell into a heavy silence as the gravity of the situation settled upon them. Outside, the sounds of the city continued, but the tension in the air was palpable. War was coming, and with it, a reckoning that would change Yax Mutal forever.

The streets of Yax Mutal were alive with anxious murmurs as Balam, accompanied by Ixchel, made his way through the city. Citizens gathered in clusters, their faces filled with uncertainty and fear. Rumors of Yaxuun's betrayal had spread like wildfire, and the looming threat of Calakmul's armies weighed heavily on their minds.

As Balam approached the central square, a crowd began to form. The people of Yax Mutal, once proud and united, were now divided, torn between loyalty to their king and fear of Yaxuun's rising power.

Balam stepped onto a raised platform, his heart pounding in his chest. He could feel the eyes of the city upon him, waiting for answers, waiting for hope.

"My people," Balam began, his voice carrying across the square. "I stand before you today not as a prince, but as one of you. I know the fear that grips your hearts, the uncertainty that hangs over our city like a shadow."

The crowd shifted uneasily, their eyes fixed on Balam.

"We face threats from all sides," he continued. "From within, Yaxuun seeks to divide us, to turn us against one another. And from without, Calakmul marches upon our city, seeking to destroy all that we hold dear."

A ripple of fear passed through the crowd, but Balam pressed on.

"But we are not powerless," he said, his voice rising with determination. "We are the people of Yax Mutal! We are strong, we are united, and we will not be broken by the greed of men or the ambitions of foreign kings."

A murmur of agreement began to spread through the crowd.

"My father, the great king Jasaw Chan K'awiil I, has led this city with wisdom and strength for many years," Balam said, his voice filled with pride. "And he still stands, ready to defend Yax Mutal. But he cannot do it alone. We cannot do it alone."

Balam paused, letting his words sink in. "Now is the time for unity. Now is the time to stand together, not as divided citizens, but as one people, under one banner."

The crowd began to stir, a sense of hope kindling in their hearts.

"Yaxuun may seek to divide us, but we are stronger together," Balam declared, his voice filled with conviction. "Calakmul may march upon us, but we will meet them with the full strength of Yax Mutal. We will not let them take what is ours!"

Cheers erupted from the crowd, their fear giving way to a growing sense of determination.

As Balam looked out over the sea of faces, he knew that the battle ahead would be fierce. But for the first time, he felt the strength of the people behind him. The storm was coming, but Yax Mutal would stand strong.

Ixchel, standing at his side, felt a deep sense of pride swell within her. Balam had ignited the flame of hope in the hearts of his people. The gods had chosen well.

But as the crowd's cheers filled the air, Ixchel's mind drifted to Yaxuun. The storm was not over. It had only just begun.

Chapter 15: The Breaking of Blood

The air inside the palace felt thick, weighed down by the whispers of betrayal. Servants hurried down the stone corridors, their heads lowered, avoiding the eyes of the royal guards who stood rigid, tense. Everyone knew that the calm within the palace walls was an illusion. It was the kind of calm that came before a storm.

In the heart of the palace, Balam paced inside his chamber, his mind racing. He had just returned from the city square, where the people's spirits had been lifted by his speech. But the war wasn't only on the outside. It was inside Yax Mutal too, festering like a hidden wound. His brother, Yaxuun, was that wound.

Balam stopped and ran a hand over his face. His brother's ambition had always been clear—he coveted the throne, just as he coveted the power that came with it. And now, with Calakmul's armies on the move, Yaxuun had chosen his moment to strike. Treachery from within, invasion from without. Their enemies couldn't have timed it better.

A soft knock on the door drew Balam from his thoughts.

"Enter," he called, his voice steady but strained.

The door opened, and Ixchel stepped inside, her face drawn with concern. "Balam, it's happening. The guards... they're talking. They say Yaxuun has made his move."

Balam's jaw tightened. "What have they heard?"

Ixchel stepped closer, her voice low. "There are whispers that Yaxuun has begun rallying support among the nobles, promising them power if they help him take the throne. Some say he's already met with envoys from Calakmul."

Balam's fists clenched at his sides. He had known his brother's ambition ran deep, but to openly align with Calakmul—the sworn enemy of Yax Mutal—it was worse than he had feared.

"We must confront him before this goes any further," Balam said, his eyes darkening with resolve. "I won't let him tear this city apart."

The throne room was eerily quiet when Balam entered. At the far end of the room, beneath the towering stone effigies of the gods, Yaxuun stood, his back to the door, gazing out at the city below. His figure was cloaked in shadow, but Balam could feel the tension radiating from him, like the air before a storm.

"Brother," Balam called, his voice echoing off the stone walls.

Yaxuun didn't turn. He stood still for a long moment before finally speaking. "It's strange, isn't it?" His voice was calm, too calm. "That a city so great, so powerful, could be brought to its knees by something as simple as ambition."

Balam stepped further into the room, his eyes locked on his brother's back. "Yaxuun, you've gone too far. I know about your meetings with the nobles. I know about your promises. And I know about Calakmul."

Yaxuun turned then, slowly, his lips curling into a bitter smile. "You always were quick to see the worst in me, Balam."

Balam's jaw tightened. "I see only what you've become. This is madness, Yaxuun. You'd betray your own blood, your own city, for what? A throne? Power?"

"For survival!" Yaxuun's voice cracked like a whip as he stepped forward, his face twisted with rage. "You don't understand, Balam. You never did. Father is old, weak. Yax Mutal is crumbling, and if we don't act, Calakmul will burn this city to the ground."

THE DAWN OF THE JAGUAR

"Aligning with them won't save us," Balam shot back. "You think they'll let you rule once Yax Mutal falls? You're a pawn to them, Yaxuun, just like every other traitor they've used."

Yaxuun's eyes blazed with fury. "And what do you propose? We sit and wait for Father to die? Let you, the golden son, take the throne while I'm left with nothing?"

"This isn't about you!" Balam's voice thundered, reverberating off the walls. "This is about Yax Mutal! About our people! Don't you see? Your actions are tearing us apart."

For a moment, there was silence. The two brothers stood facing each other, the weight of years of rivalry, jealousy, and misunderstanding hanging between them like a blade.

Yaxuun's face twisted into a snarl. "You always thought you were better than me. Always so noble, so righteous. But the truth is, Balam, you're weak. You don't have the spine to do what's necessary to save this city."

Balam took a step forward, his fists clenched. "What's necessary? You mean betraying everything our father built? Everything our ancestors fought for?"

Yaxuun sneered. "You talk about the past like it's worth preserving. But Yax Mutal needs change. It needs strength. And I will give it that, whether you like it or not."

Without warning, Yaxuun lunged, drawing a dagger from his belt and slashing it toward Balam. But Balam was ready. He sidestepped the blow and grabbed his brother's wrist, twisting the blade from his hand and sending it clattering to the floor.

"Stop this, Yaxuun," Balam growled, his grip tightening. "It doesn't have to end like this."

Yaxuun struggled, his eyes wild with rage and desperation. "You're a fool, Balam! You can't stop me! You'll never stop me!"

With a surge of strength, Yaxuun wrenched free from Balam's grip and scrambled toward the door. Balam didn't follow. He stood there, breathing heavily, watching as his brother fled the throne room.

In the darkness of the jungle just outside Yax Mutal's walls, Yaxuun stood panting, his heart pounding in his chest. His clothes were torn, his face streaked with sweat and dirt. He had fled the palace, barely escaping with his life. But he was far from defeated.

Ahead of him, a small group of men awaited him—envoys from Calakmul, their eyes gleaming in the moonlight.

"Lord Yaxuun," one of them said, bowing slightly. "We've been expecting you."

Yaxuun straightened, wiping the sweat from his brow. "Take me to your king. I have much to discuss with Yuknoom Ch'een."

The envoy smiled. "As you wish, my lord. Calakmul will welcome you with open arms."

As Yaxuun followed the envoys into the jungle, a sense of grim determination settled over him. Balam had spared him tonight, but the next time they met, there would be no mercy.

Back in the palace, Balam stood in the throne room, staring at the empty space where his brother had stood just moments ago. His chest ached with the weight of what had just transpired. He had let Yaxuun go, sparing his life, but in doing so, he had allowed his brother to flee into the hands of Yax Mutal's enemies.

Ixchel appeared at the door, her eyes filled with worry. "Balam," she whispered, stepping toward him. "Are you all right?"

Balam nodded, though his heart was heavy. "I had to let him go," he said softly. "He's my brother."

THE DAWN OF THE JAGUAR

Ixchel placed a gentle hand on his arm. "I know. But now he's with Calakmul. The war isn't just on the horizon anymore—it's here."

Balam's eyes darkened with resolve as he looked toward the door, where his brother had vanished into the night. "Then we'll face it. Together."

The breaking of blood had come, but the fight for Yax Mutal was far from over.

Chapter 16: The Siege of Yax Mutal

The ground beneath Yax Mutal trembled. From the towering city walls, the people could see the smoke rising in the distance, thick and black, like the breath of some monstrous beast approaching. The war drums of Calakmul echoed across the valley, their deep, rhythmic pounding sending shivers through the bones of every man, woman, and child.

Inside the city, the atmosphere was heavy with dread, but there was also determination. The people of Yax Mutal had endured for generations, and now, in the face of one of their greatest threats, they would not surrender easily.

Balam stood atop the walls, his eyes scanning the horizon. The army of Calakmul stretched far beyond what he could see. Warriors dressed in fierce jaguar pelts and painted with war symbols marched forward, their obsidian weapons gleaming in the sunlight. Among them, banners waved, carrying the symbol of K'ahk' Tiliw Chan Chaak, the ruthless general leading the siege.

"They're coming in greater numbers than we expected," said one of Balam's commanders, his voice grim.

Balam nodded, his expression hardening. "We knew this day would come. We're ready."

Behind him, Ixchel stood, her eyes closed in deep concentration. Ever since their return to Yax Mutal, she had been plagued by more visions, flashes of the jaguar god, of flames consuming the city, and of blood soaking the earth. The gods had spoken to her in the cenote, and though their messages were often cryptic, she had come to understand one thing clearly: Yax Mutal's survival depended not just on brute strength but on divine guidance.

"Balam," she said softly, opening her eyes. "The tunnels beneath the city... they are the key."

Balam turned to her, frowning. "Tunnels? What do you mean?"

"In my visions," she explained, "I saw a hidden path. Beneath the city, there are ancient tunnels that were dug by our ancestors long ago, forgotten by most. The gods showed them to me for a reason. We can use them to strike from within the earth, to catch Calakmul off guard."

Balam's eyes lit up with realization. The city's defense had always focused on its towering walls and strong gates, but beneath Yax Mutal, an unseen advantage lay waiting to be discovered. "If these tunnels are still intact, they could be our only hope."

He turned to his commander. "Gather a small group of our best men. We're going underground."

As the people of Yax Mutal prepared for war, the city buzzed with frantic energy. Women carried baskets of food and water to the warriors at the front lines, while priests gathered in the temples to pray for divine protection. The air was thick with the scent of incense and the sound of prayers.

Ixchel, now recognized by many as a prophetess of the gods, stood before a group of citizens in the central plaza. Her once-humble presence now commanded attention, and the people looked to her for guidance.

"People of Yax Mutal," she began, her voice carrying across the plaza, "we stand on the edge of destruction, but the gods have not forsaken us. They have shown me the way, and they have given us a weapon that Calakmul cannot see."

The crowd murmured, their eyes wide with a mixture of fear and hope.

"We have tunnels beneath this city," Ixchel continued, "ancient paths that our ancestors once used. With these tunnels, we can strike at our enemy from the shadows. We will not wait for them to bring war to our gates. We will bring the war to them."

A wave of determination swept through the crowd, and many began to chant her name. "Ixchel! Ixchel! Ixchel!"

As the chanting grew louder, Balam arrived at the plaza, leading a group of warriors. He paused for a moment, watching as Ixchel rallied the people. A sense of pride welled up within him. She had grown from the frightened girl who had once sought his help into a powerful leader, a voice for the gods.

He approached her, placing a hand on her shoulder. "It's time."

Beneath the city, the air was damp and thick with the smell of earth. The tunnels were narrow, barely wide enough for two men to walk side by side. Balam led the way, his torch flickering in the darkness, casting eerie shadows on the stone walls. Behind him, Ixchel walked with a determined expression, her heart pounding in her chest. This was what the gods had shown her, but now that they were here, the weight of what was to come pressed heavily on her shoulders.

As they moved deeper into the labyrinth, the sounds of the battle above grew faint, replaced by the soft drip of water echoing in the distance. The tunnel twisted and turned, but Ixchel guided them with confidence. She knew this path, not from memory but from the visions that had been burned into her mind.

At last, they came to a wide chamber, where several passages converged. Balam raised his torch, illuminating the space. "This is it," he said. "We're beneath the enemy's camp."

He turned to the warriors behind him, their faces grim but resolute. "We'll split into two groups. One will sabotage their supply lines, the other will create chaos in their ranks. We strike fast and we strike hard. By the time they realize what's happening, it will be too late."

The men nodded, gripping their weapons tightly. Balam met Ixchel's gaze, his expression serious. "Stay here. If anything goes wrong, return to the city through the tunnels."

Ixchel shook her head. "I'm coming with you."

Balam hesitated, but he knew there was no point in arguing. Ixchel had proven herself time and time again. "Then stay close."

Above ground, the siege had begun. Calakmul's warriors pressed against Yax Mutal's gates, hurling burning torches and battering rams. The city's defenders fought fiercely, pouring boiling water and stones down on their enemies, but the sheer number of attackers was overwhelming.

Just as it seemed the gates might give way, a sudden explosion rocked the battlefield. A column of fire shot up from Calakmul's camp, followed by the sound of screams and chaos. Warriors scrambled in confusion as another explosion shook the ground, this one closer to their supply lines.

From the hidden tunnels beneath the earth, Balam's men emerged, striking like shadows. They cut through Calakmul's forces with precision, sabotaging their supplies, setting fires, and spreading panic. In the midst of the chaos, Balam led a small group directly into the heart of the enemy camp.

The general of Calakmul, K'ahk' Tiliw Chan Chaak, stood at the center, barking orders at his men. He had not expected such an attack, not from beneath the ground. As he turned to regroup his forces, he saw Balam charging toward him, his obsidian sword raised.

"You!" K'ahk' Tiliw snarled, drawing his own weapon. "You think you can stop Calakmul?"

Balam didn't answer. He swung his blade, and the two clashed in a fierce battle. Around them, the sounds of war raged on, but in that moment, it was just the two of them—warrior against warrior, city against city.

The duel was brutal, each man landing blow after blow, but in the end, it was Balam who emerged victorious. With one final strike, he disarmed the general and brought him to his knees.

K'ahk' Tiliw glared up at Balam, blood trickling from his lips. "This won't stop us," he hissed. "Calakmul will return. We will always return."

Balam's eyes hardened. "Not this time."

With a swift motion, he ended the general's life.

Back in Yax Mutal, the tide of the battle had turned. The defenders, emboldened by the chaos in the enemy's camp, pushed forward, driving Calakmul's forces back. The invaders, now leaderless and disoriented, began to retreat, their once mighty siege crumbling.

As the last of Calakmul's warriors fled into the jungle, a cheer rose up from the walls of Yax Mutal. The city had survived, not through strength alone, but through the wisdom of its people and the guidance of the gods.

Exhausted but triumphant, Balam and Ixchel stood at the gates, watching as the remnants of their enemy disappeared into the distance.

"It's over," Ixchel whispered, her voice filled with relief.

Balam nodded, though he knew the battle might be over, but the war was far from finished. "For now."

As the sun set over the city, casting its golden light on the ancient stones, Balam and Ixchel shared a look of understanding. They had faced the darkness together, and though the future was uncertain, they knew one thing for sure: Yax Mutal had been given a second chance.

And they would do everything in their power to protect it.

Chapter 17: Signs from the Sky

The sky above Yax Mutal was no longer a tranquil blue, but a strange, shifting canvas of colors. Unnatural hues—blood-red, violet, and deep, stormy gray—swirled in eerie patterns, almost as if the heavens themselves were in turmoil. The people of Yax Mutal looked upward with wide eyes, murmuring amongst themselves, sensing that something beyond the realm of men had begun to stir.

High above the city, on the temple platform of the Great Pyramid, the priests gathered. The air was thick with the scent of burning copal incense, and the rhythmic sound of drums reverberated through the sacred grounds. King Jasaw Chan K'awiil I stood among them, staring at the sky, his face grim and lined with worry. He had faced many battles in his life, had ruled over his people with strength and wisdom, but this—this was something new. Something far beyond his understanding.

"The gods are speaking," said Ah Kin Chi, the high priest, his voice solemn. He turned to the king. "Their anger has not been soothed by our offerings. These signs..." He pointed to the sky, where a streak of lightning, glowing an unnatural green, cracked across the horizon. "They are omens of destruction. If we do not act, Yax Mutal may be doomed."

Jasaw clenched his fists at his sides. "We have defended our city against the forces of Calakmul. Our warriors are strong, and the people are united. How can this be? How can the gods turn against us now?"

Ah Kin Chi sighed. "It is not strength alone that will save us, my king. We are entangled in the web of fate, spun by the gods themselves. Our survival may no longer be in our hands."

A sudden gust of wind blew across the platform, causing the torches to flicker and the priests' robes to flutter. From the city below, the sound of gasps and murmurs grew louder as the people pointed at the sky once more. A massive, fiery shape was forming in the clouds—an unmistakable figure.

"The jaguar god," whispered one of the younger priests, his voice trembling with fear.

Indeed, the outline of a jaguar's head, with blazing eyes and sharp, gleaming teeth, seemed to emerge from the storm clouds. Its form twisted and moved, as if alive, prowling through the heavens.

In the heart of the city, Ixchel and Balam stood among the people, watching the terrifying apparition unfold above them. Ixchel's heart pounded in her chest as she clutched her obsidian pendant, a gift from her mother, for protection.

"This is what I saw in my visions," she whispered to Balam, her voice shaking. "The jaguar god has come to pass judgment."

Balam stared up at the sky, his face unreadable, but his hand tightened around the hilt of his sword. He was a man of action, a warrior, and yet, here, in the face of the divine, he felt helpless. "We can fight armies," he said quietly, "but how do we fight the gods?"

Ixchel shook her head. "We don't. We must understand their will, and find a way to appease them. We've followed the path the gods laid before us so far, but now... now, I fear something darker is coming."

As if in response to her words, the jaguar god's fiery eyes turned downward, fixing on the city of Yax Mutal. The clouds rumbled, and a wave of unnatural heat washed over the city, causing the people to cry out in terror. The ground trembled, and buildings shook as though some great force was pressing down upon them.

"Look!" someone shouted from the crowd.

Balam and Ixchel followed the direction of the voice, and what they saw chilled them to the bone. In the distance, over the hills beyond Yax Mutal, a new army was assembling—Calakmul's forces. But there

THE DAWN OF THE JAGUAR

was something unnatural about the way they moved, as though driven by something more than mortal ambition. Shadows seemed to swirl around them, and strange, glowing shapes flitted through the air above them—spirits, or perhaps the vengeful gods themselves.

"We need to speak to the priests," Balam said, his voice firm. "If the gods are truly involved in this war, we need to understand their will, before it's too late."

In the sacred chambers beneath the Great Pyramid, Balam and Ixchel knelt before Ah Kin Chi. The high priest sat in silence, his eyes closed, as if listening to something far beyond the mortal world. The flickering light from the torches cast long, wavering shadows across the stone walls, making the chamber feel even more ominous.

Ixchel could feel the weight of the gods pressing down on her, their presence almost suffocating. She looked up at the high priest, her voice trembling. "We've seen the jaguar god in the sky, just as I saw in my visions. What do the gods want from us?"

Ah Kin Chi opened his eyes slowly, his gaze heavy with sorrow. "The gods are angry, but their wrath is not only directed at Calakmul. Yax Mutal is not blameless in their eyes. We have grown proud, corrupt. The blood spilled in this war has stained the earth, and the gods demand retribution."

Balam's jaw clenched. "What must we do? How can we save our city?"

The priest shook his head. "There is no easy answer, young prince. The gods require sacrifice, but not in the way we have come to understand it. They do not want more bloodshed. They want balance."

Ixchel's eyes widened. "Balance? What kind of balance?"

Ah Kin Chi rose to his feet, moving toward a large stone altar in the center of the chamber. Upon it lay a golden mask, encrusted with jade and feathers. The mask of the jaguar god. "The gods require a bridge between the worlds," the priest said quietly. "A connection between the mortal and the divine. They are testing us, to see if we are worthy of that balance. If we fail, Yax Mutal will fall."

Ixchel and Balam exchanged a glance. The weight of the priest's words hung in the air like a heavy stone. "And if we succeed?" Balam asked.

The priest looked at him, his face grave. "Then Yax Mutal may yet stand. But the cost will be great. The gods demand not only sacrifice, but unity. The two cities—Yax Mutal and Calakmul—must find a way to come together, or both will be destroyed."

Balam stared at the priest in disbelief. "You're asking for peace? After all the bloodshed, after everything Calakmul has done to our people? How can we make peace with them?"

"The gods see beyond our petty conflicts," Ah Kin Chi said. "They care not for the pride of men. The war between Yax Mutal and Calakmul is nothing compared to the war between the mortal and the divine. If we do not set aside our differences, we will all be swept away."

As Balam and Ixchel left the sacred chambers, the sky above Yax Mutal continued to churn with ominous signs. The jaguar god's fiery form loomed larger, casting a shadow over the city. The drums of Calakmul's army echoed in the distance, growing closer with each passing moment.

Balam's heart was heavy as he led Ixchel through the crowded streets. The people looked to him for hope, for guidance, but how could he lead them when the gods themselves were against them? How could he ask his father, his people, to consider peace with their greatest enemy?

Beside him, Ixchel walked in silence, her face pale and drawn. The weight of the gods' will pressed heavily on her as well. She had seen the future in her visions, had glimpsed the destruction that was to come. But she had also seen something else—something that gave her hope.

THE DAWN OF THE JAGUAR

"The gods have tested us before," she said softly, breaking the silence. "They tested our ancestors, and they survived. We can survive too, if we're willing to listen."

Balam glanced at her, his brow furrowed. "And what do you think the gods want from us, Ixchel?"

She looked up at the sky, where the jaguar god's fiery eyes glowed with divine fury. "I think they want us to learn. To understand that strength is not enough. That power is not enough. They want us to remember that we are all connected, even to those we consider our enemies."

Balam was silent for a long moment, considering her words. Then he nodded. "I hope you're right, Ixchel. For all our sakes."

As the two of them walked back toward the palace, the sky above Yax Mutal darkened further, and the first stars began to appear—strange, unfamiliar constellations that glittered with an otherworldly light.

The gods were watching.

Chapter 18: Brothers at War

The drums of war pounded like the heartbeat of a great beast, shaking the very ground beneath Yax Mutal. The sun, now hidden behind thick storm clouds, cast an eerie twilight over the battlefield, where two armies stood face-to-face, separated only by a thin stretch of open land. On one side, the warriors of Yax Mutal, battered but unbroken, stood behind their prince, Balam, the youngest son of King Jasaw Chan K'awiil I. On the other side, the vast army of Calakmul, with its banners of black and gold fluttering ominously in the wind, was led by none other than Yaxuun—Balam's elder brother.

Balam stood at the front of his troops, his obsidian-edged sword gleaming in his hand. His body was weary, his mind clouded by exhaustion, but his heart beat steady with purpose. He had known this day would come, ever since Yaxuun's betrayal had been exposed. He had hoped—prayed, even—that his brother might reconsider, that there might be some shred of love or loyalty left in him. But now, as he gazed across the battlefield and saw Yaxuun standing proudly in the armor of Calakmul, all hope of reconciliation faded.

"Today, it ends," Balam whispered to himself.

Ixchel stood beside him, her eyes scanning the horizon with a mix of dread and resolve. The visions had shown her this moment—this confrontation between brothers—and though she had tried to change the course of fate, it seemed inevitable. The jaguar god had spoken through her dreams, and now his will would be carried out.

"Balam," she said softly, placing a hand on his arm. "You don't have to fight him."

Balam glanced at her, his expression hard but grateful for her presence. "I do," he replied. "This is more than just a battle between cities. This is between us—between the blood that binds us. He won't stop until Yax Mutal is ashes, and if I don't stand in his way, who will?"

Ixchel's heart ached for him, but she knew there was no stopping what was to come. "The jaguar god is with you," she said. "I feel it. Trust in his strength."

Balam nodded, though inside, he wasn't sure what that meant anymore. The gods had shown themselves in strange and terrifying ways over the past days—omens in the sky, whispers in the wind, visions that blurred the line between the mortal and divine. Could he truly trust the jaguar god? Or was he just a pawn in some greater cosmic game?

Across the field, Yaxuun surveyed the battlefield with cold, calculating eyes. He stood atop his war chariot, the crest of Calakmul rising proudly above him. His armor, decorated with golden feathers and obsidian jewels, glinted in the dying light. This was his moment. He had always been destined for greatness, and now he would prove it—not as a prince of Yax Mutal, but as a general of Calakmul.

"Brother," Yaxuun muttered under his breath, his lips curling into a smirk. "I knew you would be foolish enough to face me."

He had discarded any sense of loyalty or familial love long ago. Balam was nothing more than an obstacle—a weak, sentimental fool clinging to a dying city. Yaxuun would burn Yax Mutal to the ground and claim his rightful place as a conqueror. The gods favored the strong, and he would prove himself worthy of their favor by crushing his brother beneath his heel.

Turning to his second-in-command, a grim-faced warrior named Ik'tan, Yaxuun gestured toward the enemy lines. "Prepare the men. We'll break through their front within the hour."

THE DAWN OF THE JAGUAR

Ik'tan nodded but hesitated for a moment, his gaze lingering on Yaxuun. "My lord," he said carefully, "there are... strange omens in the sky. The men are uneasy. They say the gods are watching."

Yaxuun's smirk faded into a sneer. "The gods?" he scoffed. "The gods are nothing more than stories to keep the weak in line. We are the masters of our own fate. If the men are frightened, tell them to fear me more than any ghost in the sky."

Ik'tan bowed, though he didn't seem entirely convinced, and went to relay the orders.

Yaxuun turned his gaze back to the distant figure of Balam, standing tall amidst his warriors. For a moment, a flicker of something—perhaps regret—crossed his features. But it was gone as quickly as it came.

"Let's see if you still have the heart of a prince, little brother," Yaxuun muttered as he drew his sword.

The two armies surged toward each other, a tidal wave of warriors clashing in the middle of the battlefield. The sound of metal on metal rang out, accompanied by the cries of the wounded and the battle chants of the warriors. The ground shook with the weight of the struggle, and the air was thick with the scent of blood and sweat.

Balam fought at the front of his troops, his sword slicing through the enemy with precision and strength. Every strike, every movement felt guided, as though something greater than himself was moving through him. The jaguar god's presence was strong now, coursing through his veins like fire.

He could feel the eyes of the gods upon him. The jaguar god was watching, waiting.

Across the battlefield, Yaxuun cut his way through Balam's forces with brutal efficiency. His sword flashed in the dim light, and his warriors followed his lead, carving a path of destruction through the ranks of Yax Mutal.

And then, through the chaos, the two brothers saw each other.

For a moment, time seemed to stop. The battlefield around them faded into the background as their eyes locked. There was no escape from this confrontation. It had always been leading to this.

With a roar, Yaxuun charged at Balam, his sword raised high.

Balam stood his ground, his grip tightening on his weapon. He felt the jaguar god stir within him, urging him forward.

The clash of their blades echoed across the battlefield as they met in the center of the fray. Sparks flew from their weapons, and the force of their blows reverberated through the ground. They fought with a fury born of years of rivalry, of wounds both physical and emotional.

"Why do you fight for a dying city?" Yaxuun spat, his voice filled with venom as he swung his sword at Balam. "Yax Mutal is finished! Calakmul will rise, and you could stand at my side, but instead, you choose to die with them."

Balam blocked the strike and pushed Yaxuun back. "You're wrong, brother," he said, his voice calm despite the chaos around them. "Yax Mutal isn't dying. It's changing. The gods have spoken, and they demand balance, not destruction."

"The gods?" Yaxuun sneered. "I serve no gods but my own strength. You're a fool, Balam, clinging to your visions and your omens. Strength is all that matters in this world. And I will prove it by ending you."

With a guttural cry, Yaxuun attacked again, his strikes becoming more wild, more desperate. But something had changed in Balam. He no longer fought out of anger or fear. He fought with purpose, with a sense of destiny guiding his every move.

And then, in a moment of pure clarity, Balam felt it—the presence of the jaguar god, stronger than ever before. It was as though the god had taken form within him, moving through him, guiding his hand.

THE DAWN OF THE JAGUAR

His eyes seemed to glow with an inner light, and his movements became fluid, almost otherworldly.

Yaxuun faltered, his eyes widening as he saw the change in his brother. "What... what are you?"

Balam didn't answer. With one final strike, he disarmed Yaxuun, sending his sword clattering to the ground. Yaxuun stumbled back, his chest heaving, his eyes filled with disbelief.

"You're not stronger than me," Yaxuun gasped, his voice shaking. "I am the rightful ruler."

Balam stepped forward, his sword lowered but his eyes burning with resolve. "This isn't about who's stronger, Yaxuun. This is about the future of our people. The gods demand balance. You've lost yourself in your thirst for power. It's over."

For a moment, Yaxuun stared at him, his chest rising and falling rapidly. And then, without a word, he turned and fled, disappearing into the chaos of the battlefield.

Balam watched him go, his heart heavy with sorrow. He had won the battle, but the war was far from over.

Chapter 19: Visions of Destruction and Hope

The nights in Yax Mutal had grown heavier, cloaked in an oppressive air that seemed to press down on the city like a smothering fog. In the days following Yaxuun's retreat and Calakmul's regrouping, the sense of impending doom hung over every alley and every market square. The people of Yax Mutal could feel it, a deep, unshakable unease, as if the gods themselves were watching and waiting.

And Ixchel—Ixchel felt it most of all.

She sat by the edge of a small fire in one of the hidden chambers beneath the palace, a place only the royal family and a select few trusted priests knew of. Her fingers traced the ancient carvings along the stone walls, depicting scenes of gods and men, battles and rituals. She closed her eyes, but even in the darkness behind her eyelids, the visions came.

The city in flames.

Jaguar gods stalking the streets.

The walls crumbling into dust.

And always, at the edge of the destruction, there was a faint glimmer of something else—hope. A light, a ritual, a way to stop the coming catastrophe. But it was fleeting, and she could never quite grasp it fully before the visions faded.

Balam's footsteps echoed through the chamber as he approached. The prince had been restless since his encounter with Yaxuun. He had been forced to fight his brother, a confrontation he had never wanted. The victory, though decisive, weighed heavily on his soul. And now, with Calakmul's forces preparing to strike again, his burden seemed unbearable.

"Ixchel?" he called softly.

She turned toward him, her eyes still clouded with the remnants of her latest vision. "Balam."

He knelt beside her, his face a mask of exhaustion, concern, and quiet determination. "Have you seen anything new?"

Ixchel hesitated, unsure of how to explain the tangled threads of fate she had glimpsed. "Yes. But it's... complicated. The destruction of Yax Mutal is certain unless we can intervene. The gods have made that clear. But there is hope—there are rituals, ancient ones, that can shift the course of fate."

Balam's brow furrowed. "Rituals? What kind of rituals?"

Ixchel exhaled, feeling the weight of the prophecy settling onto her shoulders. "It's not clear yet. The visions show glimpses, fragments of something that has been forgotten over time. The jaguar god has appeared to me, showing me the path. But it is dangerous, Balam. The wrong step, and we could doom the city ourselves."

Balam's hand instinctively tightened around the hilt of his sword. "We're already doomed if we do nothing. Whatever it is, Ixchel, we have to try."

Her eyes met his, and in that moment, they shared the same understanding: time was running out. Calakmul's forces were already regrouping. Yaxuun would return, emboldened and vengeful. And beyond the armies, there was something greater—something divine and terrible, looming just beyond the horizon.

"I need to speak to the high priests," Ixchel said firmly. "They know the ancient texts better than anyone. We must uncover the full ritual. The gods demand balance, and we can restore it—but we need their guidance."

Balam nodded. "I'll take you to them. But they're... skeptical of you, Ixchel. You're still seen as an outsider, a girl with strange powers, and many of them distrust your connection to the gods."

"I know," she said, her voice steady. "But they will listen if you stand beside me."

THE DAWN OF THE JAGUAR

In the dimly lit hall of the high priests, the air was thick with incense and the murmurs of old men in robes, gathered around an ancient altar. The high priest, Ah Kin Chi, stood at the center, his expression unreadable as he listened to Ixchel's plea.

"The gods have shown me what must be done," Ixchel said, her voice strong but filled with urgency. "Yax Mutal's destruction is near, but there is a way to stop it. There is a ritual—an ancient ritual lost to time, but one that can restore balance."

The high priests exchanged uneasy glances. Ah Kin Chi, the eldest and most respected among them, stepped forward. His face, lined with age and wisdom, bore the weight of countless years of service to the gods.

"And you, a young girl from the outskirts, claim to know the will of the gods better than we who have served them all our lives?" Ah Kin Chi's voice was soft but carried the power of authority.

Balam stepped forward, his hand resting on Ixchel's shoulder. "She has seen things none of us can deny. I've seen them too, in my own dreams. The jaguar god speaks to her, and we cannot ignore it."

Ah Kin Chi's gaze shifted to Balam, and for a moment, the tension in the room was palpable. The high priest's eyes narrowed. "Dreams can be deceiving, Prince Balam. And the gods... they are not always kind. They test us. They tempt us."

Ixchel took a deep breath, knowing this was the moment she had to convince them. "The gods are testing us, yes," she said. "But they are also offering a path to salvation. The city's fate is not set in stone—there is still time. The jaguar god has shown me glimpses of the rituals, the offerings we must make to restore balance. But I need your help to understand them fully."

The silence in the room was deafening. The high priests were not easily swayed, and Ixchel could feel their skepticism bearing down on her. But then, after what felt like an eternity, Ah Kin Chi spoke again.

"There are old texts," he said slowly, "scrolls that speak of the rituals you mention. They are ancient, nearly forgotten, and dangerous. The gods do not give their blessings without great sacrifice."

Ixchel's heart skipped a beat. "What kind of sacrifice?"

Ah Kin Chi's gaze turned grave. "Blood, child. The gods demand blood. Always. The balance you seek to restore is not without cost. To avert the city's destruction, the ritual will require an offering... and it must come from the royal line."

Balam stiffened beside her. "You mean my father."

"Or you," the high priest said, his eyes fixed on Balam. "The gods have already shown their favor to you, Balam. If the jaguar god truly walks with you, then it may be you they demand as the offering."

A heavy silence followed his words. Ixchel felt the weight of the prophecy settling over them all, the enormity of what lay ahead.

"There must be another way," Balam said, his voice low but resolute. "I'll give my life if it means saving Yax Mutal, but we need to be certain."

"The texts will tell us more," Ah Kin Chi said. "We must consult them carefully, and with haste."

Ixchel looked to Balam, her heart aching at the thought of what might be required. She had seen glimpses of this in her visions—the blood, the sacrifice—but she had hoped it would not come to this.

"We'll find the way," she whispered to him. "There is still hope."

But as the high priests moved to retrieve the ancient scrolls, and as the shadows deepened in the room, Ixchel couldn't shake the feeling that the gods were watching them closely—and that whatever path they chose, the price would be high.

Chapter 20: The Breaking of the Bloodline

The sound of battle echoed across the fields just beyond the great stone walls of Yax Mutal. Dust and blood mingled in the air as the warriors of Calakmul and Yax Mutal clashed under the oppressive weight of the afternoon sun. For days, the siege had raged, but today—today would decide the fate of the city.

Balam, his armor stained with the blood of countless foes, stood at the forefront of his warriors. His breath came in heavy, ragged gasps, his muscles burning from the strain of constant combat. Yet, his mind was clear, sharpened by the weight of the prophecy he carried with him.

He knew this was the moment. Yaxuun had returned, leading the armies of Calakmul, and they would meet in battle, as the gods had foretold. But Balam also knew something darker—something he had not shared with Ixchel or the high priests. The prophecy was not only about the city's survival, but about the breaking of the royal bloodline.

His bloodline.

Across the battlefield, Yaxuun's figure appeared, his once noble face twisted with hatred and ambition. His armor gleamed in the sunlight, a stark contrast to Balam's worn and battered appearance. They locked eyes, and in that moment, Balam knew that their fates were intertwined in ways neither could escape.

"Brother!" Yaxuun's voice boomed across the field, carried by the wind and the chaos of battle. "Come face me! Or do you cower behind your walls like a dog?"

Balam's grip tightened on the hilt of his sword. He could feel the weight of the jaguar god's presence within him, a powerful, almost overwhelming force. This was the moment of truth—the moment he had seen in his visions. But even now, standing on the precipice of destiny, Balam's heart ached.

Yaxuun had once been his brother. They had grown up together, trained together, shared the same dreams of glory for Yax Mutal. But the years had twisted Yaxuun's soul, consumed by ambition and jealousy. And now, they stood on opposite sides of a battle that neither had ever truly wanted.

"Yaxuun!" Balam called out, stepping forward from his warriors, his voice calm but carrying the weight of all their shared history. "It doesn't have to be this way! We can still end this without more bloodshed. Come back to Yax Mutal, and we can rebuild together."

Yaxuun's eyes flashed with anger. "Rebuild? Rebuild under you? You, the favored son, the one chosen by the gods? No, brother. Yax Mutal will be mine. And you—you will die today."

With a roar, Yaxuun charged forward, his sword gleaming in the light. Balam braced himself, raising his own weapon to meet the attack. Their swords clashed with a deafening ring, the force of the impact sending shockwaves through both men.

The battle around them seemed to fade as the two brothers engaged in a deadly dance, each strike filled with years of buried resentment and unspoken pain. Yaxuun fought with reckless abandon, his movements fueled by rage and desperation, while Balam's strikes were precise, measured, as if every movement carried the weight of the prophecy.

"You were always jealous," Balam said between strikes, his voice strained but steady. "You always thought I was the favored one. But this isn't about power, Yaxuun! It's about the city. It's about our people!"

Yaxuun snarled, his eyes wild. "You were always the better one in their eyes! Father's chosen, the warrior prince. But where was your strength when I needed it? When I was cast aside? I will take what should have been mine!"

THE DAWN OF THE JAGUAR

Balam blocked another furious strike, his heart heavy with grief. He could see the madness in Yaxuun's eyes, the way his brother had been consumed by his own ambition. And he knew, deep down, that there was no saving him now.

With a final, powerful swing, Balam knocked Yaxuun's sword from his hand, sending it flying across the battlefield. Yaxuun stumbled back, breathing heavily, his chest heaving with exertion and fury.

"Please, Yaxuun," Balam said, his voice barely above a whisper. "Don't make me do this. You're still my brother."

But Yaxuun's eyes burned with hatred, and with a scream of rage, he lunged at Balam, his hands reaching for his brother's throat. In that split second, Balam made the decision—the decision the gods had forced upon him.

With a swift, fluid motion, Balam drove his sword into Yaxuun's chest, the blade sinking deep into flesh and bone. Yaxuun gasped, his body going rigid as the life drained from him. His eyes, wide with shock, met Balam's for a final, fleeting moment of clarity.

"Brother..." Yaxuun whispered, his voice weak, almost childlike. And then, as quickly as it had begun, it was over.

Balam held his brother's lifeless body in his arms, his heart breaking as he realized what he had done. The prophecy had been fulfilled. The royal bloodline had been broken.

But at what cost?

The battlefield had gone eerily silent, as if the world itself had paused to witness the tragedy. Balam gently lowered Yaxuun's body to the ground, his eyes filled with grief. He could feel the eyes of his warriors upon him, but he paid them no mind. This was his burden to bear, his sacrifice.

From the distant hills, the jaguar god appeared in his vision once again, watching with inscrutable eyes. Balam felt the weight of the god's presence, but this time, there was no sense of triumph. Only sadness. The god had demanded a price, and Balam had paid it.

Suddenly, a figure appeared beside him, her presence like a breath of wind cutting through the stillness. Ixchel knelt beside Balam, her eyes filled with understanding and sorrow. She had seen this too, in her visions, but knowing it had not lessened the pain.

"It had to be done," she said softly, placing a hand on Balam's shoulder. "The gods demanded it."

Balam shook his head, his voice hoarse with emotion. "I killed my own brother. How can the gods ask for this? How can they expect this to save Yax Mutal?"

Ixchel's gaze softened. "The gods are not always kind, Balam. But they see beyond what we can. Yaxuun's death... it was part of the balance. The royal bloodline had to be broken for the city to survive. It is a sacrifice—your sacrifice. And without it, the city would have been lost."

Balam closed his eyes, his hands trembling as the weight of her words sank in. He had fulfilled the prophecy, but the cost had been far greater than he had ever imagined.

The skies above darkened, and a strange silence filled the air, as if the gods themselves were mourning the loss of Yaxuun, of the royal bloodline, and of the innocence that had been stripped from Balam in that moment.

But somewhere, deep within him, Balam knew Ixchel was right. His brother's death had not been in vain. The gods had demanded balance, and now, perhaps, Yax Mutal stood a chance.

"We must finish this," Balam said finally, his voice resolute but heavy with sorrow. "For Yax Mutal. For our people."

Ixchel nodded, her hand still resting on his shoulder as they stood together, side by side, beneath the darkening sky. The jaguar god watched from the shadows, silent and still, waiting for the final act of the prophecy to unfold.

And as the winds of fate swirled around them, Balam knew that the hardest part was yet to come.

Chapter 21: The Jaguar's Summoning

The steps of the Great Pyramid stretched endlessly before Ixchel as she climbed, her bare feet feeling the cold, worn stone beneath them. The air was thick with tension and the smell of incense, swirling around her like a heavy shroud. The sky above was bruised with storm clouds, the oppressive weight of the gods' judgment looming over Yax Mutal.

At her side, Balam ascended as well, his movements deliberate but burdened. The events of the past days had weighed on him—his brother's death, the prophecy's cruel fulfillment, and the endless siege by Calakmul's forces that tightened like a noose around the city. His people looked to him for leadership, but the sacrifice demanded by the gods had left him feeling hollow.

They reached the summit of the pyramid, the heart of Yax Mutal's spiritual power, the very place where Ixchel had once seen the jaguar god in her vision. The massive altar stood before them, stained by centuries of rituals, sacrifices, and prayers. And now, it was her turn. It was her duty to summon the power of the gods, to invoke the jaguar god Balam, for the final intervention.

She took a deep breath, steadying herself. She was no longer the simple girl from the village. She was a priestess now, a vessel of the gods' will, chosen to enact the ancient rituals that would decide the fate of the city. Her visions had led her here, to this moment, where the fate of Yax Mutal, its people, and its future would be sealed.

"The time has come, Balam," she said softly, her voice carried away by the winds that howled at the pyramid's peak. "We must do this. The gods will not wait any longer."

Balam nodded, his face a mask of determination, though his eyes revealed the conflict within. He placed a hand on her shoulder, the weight of his trust palpable.

"Ixchel," he said, his voice rough from exhaustion. "I will stand by you, no matter the cost. But are you certain this will work? That the gods will listen?"

Ixchel met his gaze, her heart steady with the knowledge that had come to her in her visions. "The gods have already spoken, Balam. They have demanded blood and balance, and now they will demand more. But if we perform the rituals, if we call upon the jaguar god, he will come. He must come."

Together, they walked to the altar, where a bowl of sacred offerings lay waiting—obsidian shards, feathers of the quetzal, and the blood of the sacrifices already made. A group of priests surrounded the altar, their faces hidden behind ornate masks carved in the shapes of serpents and birds. Their low chants filled the air, creating an eerie, pulsating rhythm that seemed to mirror the heartbeat of the city itself.

As Ixchel approached the center of the altar, one of the priests, an old man with hollow eyes and a voice like gravel, stepped forward. He held a ceremonial dagger, its blade gleaming with an unnatural light.

"It is time, priestess," the old man intoned. "The gods await your summons."

Ixchel took the dagger, feeling its cold weight in her hands. She looked up at the sky, where distant lightning crackled in the clouds. The jaguar god was watching. She could feel his presence, just beyond the veil of the physical world, waiting for her call. Her heart raced, but she knew what had to be done.

"The blood of kings has been spilled," she whispered, her voice barely audible over the chants. "The bloodline has been broken."

Balam, standing beside her, clenched his fists. He had already given everything—his brother, his future, his very soul. But now, there was one final step.

THE DAWN OF THE JAGUAR

"We offer this city," Ixchel continued, "its people, its warriors, and its king. We offer all in exchange for salvation."

Balam's breath hitched, but he remained silent. This was the moment they had feared, the moment that would determine if Yax Mutal would stand or fall. And it all rested on the gods now.

Ixchel raised the dagger, her eyes fixed on the sky. The storm clouds churned above, the air growing thick with the scent of rain and the weight of something divine. She closed her eyes, feeling the power surge through her, the jaguar god's essence coursing in her veins.

"Balam," she whispered, "the time has come."

He stepped forward, understanding what must happen. He had accepted his role in the prophecy, but it did not make the moment any easier. He knelt before Ixchel, his eyes solemn but resolute.

"The blood of kings," she murmured, "must be offered freely."

Balam met her gaze, his voice steady. "For Yax Mutal."

Ixchel's hand trembled as she brought the dagger to his palm, drawing a thin line of blood. It was not the final sacrifice the gods demanded, but a symbolic one—a gesture that would open the way between the mortal and divine realms.

As Balam's blood dripped onto the altar, the winds howled louder, and the sky above seemed to shudder. The priests' chants grew more intense, their voices rising to a fevered pitch. The jaguar god was near.

Ixchel placed her hand over Balam's, their blood mingling on the sacred stone. She lifted her arms toward the heavens, her voice rising above the storm.

"Jaguar god of Yax Mutal!" she cried, her voice carrying across the city. "We summon you! Hear our plea! We offer the blood of kings, the lives of warriors, and the souls of this city! Come forth and deliver us from destruction!"

The air grew thick with power, and the ground beneath their feet trembled. Lightning cracked across the sky, illuminating the storm in flashes of white light. And then, from the depths of the clouds, a great roar echoed—low, guttural, and filled with a primal rage.

Balam stood, his eyes wide as he saw the impossible. From the swirling storm clouds, the shape of a jaguar materialized, massive and terrifying, its eyes glowing with the light of the gods. The jaguar god had answered their call.

The priests fell to their knees, their chants turning into cries of awe and fear. Ixchel stood firm, her hands still raised toward the divine beast.

"The city is yours," she whispered. "Save us."

The jaguar god leaped from the sky, its immense form descending toward the battlefield below. With each step it took, the earth shook, and the armies of Calakmul paused in their assault, their warriors staring in disbelief at the sight before them.

Balam watched, his heart pounding in his chest. The jaguar god roared again, its voice shaking the very foundations of Yax Mutal. And then, with a single, devastating leap, the god plunged into the heart of the enemy forces, tearing through their ranks with a fury that could only come from the divine.

Screams filled the air as the soldiers of Calakmul scattered, their once-mighty army crumbling before the wrath of the jaguar god. The sky lit up with fire and lightning, and Balam knew—this was the intervention they had prayed for.

Ixchel, her eyes still fixed on the scene below, felt a deep sense of peace wash over her. The city had been spared, but the price had been steep. The prophecy had come true in ways she hadn't fully anticipated, but Yax Mutal had been saved.

As the jaguar god vanished into the storm, leaving only silence and the scent of rain in its wake, Balam turned to her, his face softened with gratitude and sorrow.

"You did it," he whispered, his voice filled with awe.

THE DAWN OF THE JAGUAR

"We did it," she corrected, taking his hand in hers. "But the gods always take their due, Balam. We can only hope it's enough."

And as the first drops of rain fell upon the bloodied fields of Yax Mutal, the two of them stood together, knowing the gods had answered—and knowing their city had been forever changed.

Chapter 22: The Jaguar's Price

The drums of war echoed across the battlefield, a rhythmic pounding that seemed to shake the very bones of the earth. The once-green plains outside Yax Mutal had been transformed into a blood-soaked wasteland, where the armies of Calakmul clashed with the defenders of the city. Smoke billowed in the distance, the remnants of burning villages, and the sky was still heavy with the remnants of the storm that had carried the jaguar god to them.

Balam stood at the edge of the battlefield, his breath ragged, his body trembling with both exhaustion and power. The air around him hummed with energy, the presence of the jaguar god thrumming deep in his veins. He had seen what the god could do, had felt its presence descend upon him like a cloak of divine fury. It was overwhelming, intoxicating, but also terrifying.

The battle was reaching its peak. Calakmul's forces, led by their commander K'ahk' Tiliw Chan Chaak, had regrouped after the chaos caused by the jaguar god's appearance. Now they pressed forward with renewed vigor, knowing that if Yax Mutal fell, all the power and glory of the region would be theirs.

But Balam was not the same man who had entered this war. He had been touched by the divine, chosen by the jaguar god himself to be a vessel for his power. His heart pounded with the pulse of the beast, his muscles flexed with a strength that no human could possess. The jaguar god was within him now, urging him to act, to strike, to protect the city at any cost.

Beside him, Ixchel watched the battle unfold, her face a mixture of fear and awe. She could feel the shift in the air, the tangible presence of the gods all around them. Her visions had shown her this moment—a climactic battle where the fate of Yax Mutal would be decided. But there had been something else too, something darker, a shadow lurking just beyond the horizon.

"Balam," she called, her voice soft but urgent.

He turned to her, his eyes burning with the fire of the jaguar god. His expression was fierce, his body tense, as if every muscle was coiled and ready to spring.

"Ixchel," he said, his voice deeper than before, carrying a strange, otherworldly resonance. "The god is with me. I can feel it. The power is... beyond anything I have ever known."

She stepped closer, her hand reaching for his arm. "I know, Balam. I've seen it. But this power... it comes with a price. The gods demand balance, and the jaguar god—he won't give us this victory for free."

Balam's jaw clenched, his gaze shifting back to the battlefield where Calakmul's soldiers surged forward like a tide. His people, his warriors, were holding the line, but they were weary. The city's defenses were faltering, and without the jaguar god's strength, they would be overwhelmed.

"I don't care about the cost," Balam growled. "I will do whatever it takes to protect Yax Mutal."

Before Ixchel could respond, a war horn blared from the enemy's ranks. K'ahk' Tiliw Chan Chaak, the brutal and cunning general of Calakmul, had arrived at the front lines. His armor gleamed under the dim sunlight, and his war banners flew high, emblazoned with the symbols of his city—a snake devouring the sun.

Balam's hands flexed, his grip tightening around the hilt of his obsidian sword. The jaguar god stirred within him, a primal urge roaring to the surface. His vision blurred, and for a moment, he wasn't sure if it was him standing there, or the god itself, gazing out through his eyes.

"The god wants blood," he muttered, more to himself than to Ixchel. "And I will give it."

THE DAWN OF THE JAGUAR

He started forward, his steps heavy with purpose. Ixchel called after him, panic rising in her chest. "Balam, wait! You don't understand—"

But it was too late. The jaguar god had already taken hold.

The battlefield erupted as Balam charged into the fray. His warriors, inspired by the sight of their prince at the front, rallied behind him with cries of defiance. But it was Balam's presence—his sheer, overwhelming presence—that shook the enemy to their core.

K'ahk' Tiliw Chan Chaak spotted him immediately, recognizing the ferocity in Balam's stance, the divine aura that seemed to surround him. He barked orders to his soldiers, urging them forward, but the fear in their eyes was unmistakable.

Balam moved with the grace and speed of the jaguar, his sword slicing through the enemy like a predator tearing through its prey. He was a blur of motion, his strikes so fast and precise that the enemy soldiers barely had time to react before they fell, their blood staining the earth beneath his feet.

The jaguar god was with him.

His movements were no longer his own—they were guided by the ancient power coursing through him. He could feel the god's hunger, its primal need for violence and domination. With every kill, the power inside him grew stronger, more intoxicating. He leaped into the air, crashing down upon a group of enemy warriors, their screams cut short by the swipe of his blade.

And then he saw him—K'ahk' Tiliw Chan Chaak, standing tall at the rear of his army, his eyes locked onto Balam. The two leaders met each other's gaze across the chaos of the battlefield, and in that moment, Balam knew what had to be done.

The god demanded a sacrifice.

With a roar that echoed across the battlefield, Balam charged toward the enemy general. Soldiers scattered in his wake, too terrified to stand in his path. K'ahk' Tiliw Chan Chaak raised his shield and sword, preparing for the onslaught, but even he could not comprehend the power that was now bearing down on him.

The jaguar god was in control.

Balam's sword crashed against K'ahk' Tiliw's shield, the force of the blow sending a shockwave through the air. The enemy general staggered, but quickly regained his footing, countering with a strike aimed at Balam's side. But Balam was too fast—he moved like the wind, dodging the blow and slashing upward with his sword, cutting a deep gash into K'ahk' Tiliw's armor.

The general grunted in pain, but refused to fall. He swung again, aiming for Balam's head, but once more, the jaguar god's power guided Balam's movements, allowing him to twist out of the way. With a final, ferocious strike, Balam brought his sword down upon K'ahk' Tiliw's chest, splitting his armor and piercing his heart.

The enemy general fell to his knees, blood pouring from his wound. He looked up at Balam, his face pale and shocked, as if he couldn't believe what had just happened.

"You... you're not... human," K'ahk' Tiliw gasped.

Balam, his eyes glowing with the fire of the jaguar god, looked down at the defeated general. "No," he said quietly. "I am something more."

With one swift motion, Balam drove his sword through the general's chest, ending his life.

The battlefield fell silent as K'ahk' Tiliw Chan Chaak collapsed to the ground, dead. Calakmul's forces, seeing their leader fall, hesitated, their morale shattered. And in that moment of weakness, the warriors of Yax Mutal surged forward, driving the enemy back.

The battle was won.

But as Balam stood there, victorious, his sword dripping with blood, he felt a deep, gnawing emptiness begin to creep over him. The power of the jaguar god still surged within him, but it was no longer a blessing—it was a curse.

THE DAWN OF THE JAGUAR

Ixchel, who had watched the entire battle from the pyramid's summit, rushed to his side, her heart pounding with fear. She knew what was happening. The gods always demanded balance. The jaguar god had given them victory, but now, it would demand its price.

"Balam!" she cried, reaching for him. "You have to stop! The god is taking too much—"

But Balam couldn't hear her. The power was overwhelming, suffocating. His vision blurred, his body trembling as the jaguar god's presence grew stronger, demanding more blood, more sacrifices. He fell to his knees, clutching his head as a feral growl escaped his throat.

"The god... wants more," he gasped, his voice barely human.

Ixchel knelt beside him, tears streaming down her face. "No, Balam! You've given enough. You've given everything!"

But the jaguar god was not satisfied. It wanted the ultimate sacrifice.

As the battlefield lay quiet, and the warriors of Yax Mutal stood victorious, the sky above darkened once more. And in that moment, Balam understood the terrible truth.

To save the city, he would have to give himself to the jaguar god.

With one final, agonizing cry, Balam collapsed, the jaguar god's roar echoing across the land.

The battle was over, but the price of victory had been paid.

Chapter 23: The Crown and the Curse

The once-thundering sounds of battle had fallen to a deafening silence. The city of Yax Mutal stood, victorious but wounded, as the sun broke through the heavy clouds, casting a pale light over the blood-stained land. The victory over Calakmul had been decisive, but at what cost? The bodies of soldiers lay scattered across the field, friends and foes alike, their sacrifices now woven into the earth.

Within the walls of the great city, the mood was no better. A mournful cry echoed through the streets, a lament for those lost, but most of all for their king, Jasaw Chan K'awiil I, who now lay dying from wounds inflicted during the siege.

Balam knelt beside his father's bed in the royal chamber, his heart heavy with grief. The jaguar god's presence, once overwhelming, had receded, leaving him hollow. His body ached from the battle, but it was the weight of destiny that pressed upon him more than any physical wound. Beside him, his mother, Lady Twelve Macaw, clutched her husband's hand, her face streaked with tears.

"Balam," came a hoarse whisper from the king's lips. His voice, once strong and commanding, was now weak, barely audible above the soft rustling of the woven curtains around the bed.

"Father, I'm here," Balam said, leaning in closer. His voice was thick with emotion, torn between the joy of victory and the sorrow of impending loss.

The old king's eyes, dim but still filled with the fire of his long reign, gazed upon his son with a mixture of pride and sorrow. "The gods... have chosen you. You... are the one who must lead them now."

Balam's throat tightened. "I'm not ready, Father. There is still so much I don't understand. The prophecy—"

"The prophecy is your burden now," Jasaw interrupted, his hand shaking as he tried to grip his son's arm. "But you are strong... stronger than I ever was. The gods have marked you for greatness, but you must also be wise. Yax Mutal will need wisdom, not just strength."

Balam felt the weight of his father's words like a stone upon his chest. He had fought bravely, yes, but at what cost? The jaguar god's power had saved them, yet it had demanded something from him—something he could never take back. He could still feel its presence, lurking deep within him, waiting.

"I won't fail you, Father," Balam said quietly, his voice barely steady.

Jasaw's breath grew shallower, and his grip weakened. He looked at his son, his heir, one last time. "You are... my legacy... my greatest pride."

With that, the king's hand fell limp, his final breath leaving his body as Lady Twelve Macaw let out a wail of anguish. The priests, who had been standing nearby, lowered their heads in solemn prayer. Balam stared at his father's still form, the realization washing over him like a flood.

He was now king.

The funeral of Jasaw Chan K'awiil I was a grand affair, befitting a ruler who had defended Yax Mutal from countless threats. The entire city gathered to mourn and honor their fallen king. The funeral pyre blazed in the center of the city's grand plaza, its flames reaching high into the sky, carrying the king's spirit to the heavens. Priests chanted prayers, invoking the gods to guide him through Xibalba, the underworld, and into eternal peace.

Ixchel stood among the mourners, her eyes red from crying. She had fought beside Balam, had seen the horrors of the war, and had witnessed the price the gods had demanded. She knew what Balam was feeling—the weight of his new responsibilities, the burden of the prophecy that still loomed over him.

As the pyre burned, Balam stood at the forefront, dressed in the regal attire of a king. His new crown, adorned with jade and quetzal feathers, rested heavily on his head, though it felt more like a curse than a blessing. The people bowed before him, their new ruler, but Balam couldn't shake the feeling of dread that had settled in his chest.

After the ceremony, when the crowds had dispersed and the city grew quiet, Balam retreated to the palace, seeking solace in the solitude of his chambers. The night was still, but his mind was anything but calm. He paced the floor, his thoughts swirling.

The prophecy had been fulfilled in part—Yaxuun's death had indeed broken the royal bloodline, but what did it mean for the city? Had they truly escaped the gods' wrath, or was there more to come?

A soft knock interrupted his thoughts. He turned to see Ixchel standing in the doorway, her face full of concern.

"Balam," she said softly, stepping into the room. "You shouldn't be alone right now."

He let out a weary sigh, his shoulders slumping. "I don't know what to do, Ixchel. I thought winning the war would be enough, but…"

"It's never enough," she finished for him, moving closer. "The gods don't give us peace so easily."

He nodded, his gaze distant. "I felt the jaguar god inside me, Ixchel. It gave me strength, but it also… took something. I don't know what I am anymore."

Ixchel placed a hand on his arm, grounding him. "You are still you, Balam. But the gods have claimed a part of you. We both know this war wasn't just about the armies of Calakmul and Yax Mutal. There are forces beyond us, forces we've only begun to understand."

"I don't know if I can carry this burden," he admitted, his voice barely a whisper. "The city looks to me now, but what if I fail them? What if the gods demand more?"

Ixchel's eyes softened. "You won't fail them. You've already proven that you're willing to sacrifice everything for Yax Mutal. But you don't have to do this alone."

Balam looked at her, searching her face for some sign of reassurance. "And what about you, Ixchel? The people already whisper that you're a prophetess, that you can see the future. What do your visions show?"

She hesitated, her brow furrowing. "The future is... uncertain. I see many things, Balam. I see peace, but I also see destruction. The jaguar god's influence isn't over. The gods are still watching."

Balam clenched his fists, his frustration mounting. "Then what was all this for? Why did we fight? Why did so many die, if the gods are still not satisfied?"

Ixchel placed her hand on his chest, over his heart. "Because they believe in you. The gods gave you their strength for a reason. You can lead Yax Mutal into a new age, but only if you trust in yourself."

Balam stared at her, the weight of her words sinking in. He had always trusted in his own strength, in his ability to fight. But now, as king, he would need to rely on more than just brute force. He would need wisdom, diplomacy, and the will to face the unknown future.

"I'll try," he said finally, his voice steadying. "For my people. For Yax Mutal."

Ixchel nodded, her hand still on his heart. "We'll face whatever comes together, Balam. The gods may be watching, but so are your people. They need you now more than ever."

As the night deepened, Balam felt a flicker of hope. The path ahead was uncertain, and the prophecy still loomed over them like a shadow, but he would face it. He had to.

For Yax Mutal, for his father's legacy, and for the future he and Ixchel would build together.

The jaguar god's curse might still linger, but Balam was determined to prove that even the gods could not dictate his destiny.

Chapter 24: The Final Vision

The stars blinked faintly above Yax Mutal, as if the heavens themselves were whispering secrets that no one could hear. The city, though victorious, still carried the scars of battle. The streets were quiet now, the mourning songs of the people fading into the night. It was a strange, uneasy calm, like the breath before a storm. But in the heart of the city, within the towering palace walls, Ixchel felt anything but calm.

She sat in her small chamber, cross-legged on the floor, her eyes closed. The air around her felt thick, heavy with something unseen. Her visions had grown more intense, more frequent, and every time she closed her eyes, she saw fragments of a future she couldn't piece together. She tried to focus, to reach out to the gods who had spoken to her before, but this time was different. This time, they were calling her deeper, pulling her into a place she had never ventured.

And then, without warning, it came.

A blinding light, piercing through the darkness of her mind, and she found herself standing on the edge of a vast jungle. The trees were ancient, their branches reaching up like twisted arms, and in the distance, the outline of the Great Pyramid loomed. But the sky—there was something wrong with the sky. It was dark, not with clouds but with shadows. Above, the jaguar god's eyes burned bright, watching her.

In the vision, Ixchel felt her heart race. She was not alone.

Ahead of her, standing at the base of the pyramid, was Balam. His back was to her, and yet she knew it was him. He was dressed in the royal garb of a king, his crown shimmering in the dim light. But there was something in his stance, something weary, as if the weight of the world was upon his shoulders.

"Balam!" she called out, her voice echoing strangely in the dreamlike landscape.

He didn't turn. He didn't move.

The jaguar god roared in the sky, its voice shaking the earth beneath her feet. The ground cracked, and suddenly the scene shifted. She was no longer in the jungle. She stood at the top of the Great Pyramid, and Balam was beside her, lying on a stone altar. His face was pale, his eyes closed, and his chest was bare, marked with the ancient symbols of sacrifice.

"No!" Ixchel screamed, rushing toward him. But her feet wouldn't move. The world seemed to slow, her body paralyzed by some unseen force. She tried again, struggling to reach him, but the gods held her back.

Then, she heard the voice.

"The blood of the king will bring peace."

The words cut through the air, cold and final. Ixchel's heart sank. She understood.

Balam was the sacrifice.

The vision shattered, and Ixchel gasped as she was pulled back to the present. She was drenched in sweat, her hands trembling as she clutched at the floor. The weight of the truth settled over her like a crushing stone. The gods had shown her the way, the final piece of the prophecy.

Balam... must die.

For a long moment, she couldn't move. Her breath came in ragged gasps, her mind racing to make sense of what she had seen. It couldn't be true. Balam, the new king, the man who had saved Yax Mutal, the one destined to lead them—how could the gods demand his life?

But she knew the answer. The gods were not merciful. They had their own ways, their own rules, and they had spoken.

She had to tell him.

THE DAWN OF THE JAGUAR

With shaky legs, Ixchel rose from the floor, her heart pounding in her chest. Every step toward Balam's chambers felt heavier than the last, as if her very soul resisted what she had to do. When she reached his door, she paused, her hand hovering just above the entrance.

Would he believe her? Would he understand?

She pushed the door open.

Balam was standing at the window, gazing out over the city, his silhouette bathed in the pale moonlight. He turned when he heard her enter, a small smile on his face. "Ixchel. I was wondering where you had gone."

She forced a smile in return, but it felt wrong, like a mask she couldn't hold in place. "I... I needed to think," she said softly, stepping into the room.

Balam's smile faded as he looked at her more closely. "Something's wrong. What is it?"

Ixchel hesitated, her throat tightening. How could she tell him? How could she look him in the eyes and say that his life was the price for their peace? But she had no choice. The gods had made their will known, and she couldn't hide from it.

"Balam," she began, her voice barely a whisper, "I had another vision."

He frowned, stepping closer to her, concern etched on his face. "What did you see?"

She took a deep breath, steadying herself. "The jaguar god... it spoke to me again. It showed me the final part of the prophecy."

Balam's eyes darkened. "What did it say?"

Her lips trembled as the words left her mouth. "The only way to bring lasting peace to Yax Mutal... is through sacrifice. Your sacrifice."

For a moment, there was silence. Balam stared at her, his face unreadable, as if the words hadn't fully registered. Then, slowly, he shook his head. "No. No, that can't be right. I've fought for this city. I've saved it. The gods wouldn't—"

"The gods demand what they will," Ixchel interrupted, her voice breaking. "I saw it, Balam. I saw you. On the altar. The jaguar god has chosen you."

Balam turned away, his hands gripping the edge of the stone window ledge. His knuckles were white, his body tense. "And what if I refuse?" he asked quietly, his voice barely audible. "What if I refuse to die?"

Ixchel felt tears welling in her eyes, but she blinked them away. "If you refuse, the gods will turn their wrath on the city. Everything we've fought for, everything we've saved—it will all be for nothing. Yax Mutal will fall."

Balam's shoulders slumped, and for the first time, he looked truly defeated. He had faced armies, led his people to victory, and yet this... this was a battle he couldn't win.

"I always knew," he said softly, almost to himself. "I always knew there was something more. Something darker. The jaguar god... it's been with me since the battle. I could feel its power, but I never thought..."

Ixchel stepped closer, placing a hand on his arm. "I'm sorry, Balam. I wish there was another way. But the gods have spoken."

He turned to face her, his eyes filled with a mix of sorrow and acceptance. "And you? Do you believe this is what must happen?"

Ixchel hesitated, her heart aching. "I believe in the gods, but I also believe in you. You've given so much, Balam. I wish it didn't have to be this way."

For a long moment, neither of them spoke. The silence between them was heavy, thick with unspoken words. Then, finally, Balam nodded, a grim determination settling over his face.

"If this is the will of the gods," he said, "then I will accept it."

Ixchel's heart shattered. She had known he would say that. He was a king, after all, and a king always put his people first, even at the cost of his own life.

The prophecy would be fulfilled.

THE DAWN OF THE JAGUAR

The jaguar god's sacrifice would be made.

But the price was far greater than Ixchel had ever imagined.

As she stood there, watching Balam prepare himself for the inevitable, she realized that no victory—no matter how great—could ever come without loss.

Chapter 25: The King's Farewell

The air in Yax Mutal hung thick with anticipation, as if the city itself held its breath, knowing that something momentous was about to happen. The streets were quiet, far quieter than they had been after the victory over Calakmul. There was no celebration, no sense of triumph. The people of Yax Mutal knew their fate was tied to their king's, and Balam, their new ruler, had just days to live.

Word had spread quickly throughout the city. Balam's sacrifice was no longer a secret but a sacred truth whispered from ear to ear. Some wept, others prayed. Many simply sat in stunned silence, unable to grasp how their victory could lead to this. Their king, the warrior who had saved them, who had defended their walls and fought for their future, would soon be gone. The gods had made their will known, and there was no stopping it.

Inside the palace, Balam stood in his chamber, gazing out over the city that had been his home, his heart. The jaguar god's power still thrummed inside him, a reminder of the battle, of the divine force that had possessed him when he had faced his brother on the field. But that power, as great as it had been, came with a cost.

Balam had accepted his fate. The gods had chosen him. Now, he had to say goodbye.

Ixchel stood at the doorway, watching him. She hadn't said a word since they had spoken about the prophecy, since Balam had agreed to what the gods required of him. She had seen many sides of Balam—the thoughtful prince, the fearless warrior—but now, as he prepared for the end, she saw something she hadn't expected. A deep sadness. A quiet resignation.

He finally turned, sensing her presence. His eyes, once so full of fire, now held a calm acceptance. "You've been standing there a while," he said, his voice softer than usual.

Ixchel stepped into the room, her heart heavy with the weight of the moment. "I wanted to give you time," she replied. "Time to... process everything."

Balam gave a small, bitter smile. "Time doesn't change anything, Ixchel. We both know that." He walked toward her, his steps slow, as if each one brought him closer to an inevitable end. "But I appreciate it."

They stood in silence for a moment, the air between them thick with unspoken words. Ixchel wanted to say something, anything, to ease the burden on his shoulders, but what could she say? That she was sorry? That she wished the gods had chosen someone else? None of it would matter. The gods had spoken.

"You've done everything you could for this city," Ixchel finally said, her voice barely above a whisper. "Your people will never forget that."

Balam's gaze softened as he looked at her. "I didn't do it for them," he said. "Not entirely."

Ixchel frowned, confused. "What do you mean?"

He stepped closer, close enough that she could feel the warmth of his breath on her skin. "I did it for you."

Her heart skipped a beat. She had always known there was a bond between them, something deeper than their shared connection to the jaguar god. But to hear him say it, to know that he had fought, bled, and sacrificed for her—it was too much. Tears welled in her eyes, and she looked away, trying to keep herself together.

"Balam, don't—" she began, but he gently placed a hand on her shoulder, stopping her.

"You've given me more than you know, Ixchel," he said, his voice low and steady. "You showed me the truth, even when it was painful. You stood by me when no one else believed in the visions. You... you gave me hope, even when I had none."

THE DAWN OF THE JAGUAR

Ixchel couldn't hold back the tears any longer. They spilled down her cheeks, hot and heavy. "I didn't want this," she whispered. "I never wanted this for you."

Balam smiled sadly, brushing a tear from her face. "Neither did I. But we don't always get to choose, do we?"

The words hung in the air, filled with the weight of the choices neither of them had made. Ixchel's heart ached, knowing that this was their last moment together, the last time they would speak, the last time she would feel his warmth. She had seen so much in her visions—wars, death, destruction—but she had never seen how deeply she would feel this loss.

"We still have tonight," Balam said softly, his voice breaking the silence. "Come with me."

He led her through the palace, past the great halls and the chambers where priests and advisors whispered of the future. Outside, the stars glimmered in the night sky, clear and bright, as if the gods themselves were watching. Balam took Ixchel to the city's main plaza, where a small crowd had gathered. The people, their faces a mix of sorrow and awe, fell silent as their king appeared before them.

Balam raised his hands, his voice strong and clear as he addressed them. "People of Yax Mutal," he began, "you have fought bravely. You have endured. And because of you, our city stands."

A murmur rippled through the crowd, but no one interrupted. They listened with rapt attention, their eyes filled with respect and admiration for the man who had saved them.

Balam's voice softened, filled with a quiet strength. "The gods have spoken. They have chosen me to be the sacrifice that will ensure our city's peace. This is not a death of sorrow, but of honor. The jaguar god has protected us, and now it is my duty to offer myself in return."

The crowd remained silent, but the emotion was palpable. Some wept openly, while others clutched their children close, whispering prayers to the gods. Balam's words hung over them like a blessing and a curse.

Ixchel stood at his side, her heart breaking with every word. She had always known Balam as a warrior, a leader, but now she saw him as something more—a king who loved his people enough to die for them. His sacrifice was not just for the gods; it was for them, for the future of Yax Mutal.

After addressing the people, Balam turned to Ixchel. His eyes held hers, and for a moment, the world seemed to stop. "Will you be there?" he asked quietly, though he already knew the answer.

She nodded, her voice too choked with emotion to respond. Of course, she would be there. She had been with him every step of the way, and she would be there at the end.

Later, in the quiet of the palace, Balam sat with his advisors, preparing for the ritual that would take place at dawn. Ixchel watched from the shadows, her heart heavy with the knowledge of what was to come. She could feel the weight of the gods pressing down on her, their presence in the air around her, thick and inescapable.

As the night wore on, Balam finished his preparations. He rose from his seat, dismissing his advisors with a nod, and turned to Ixchel. They stood alone now, the silence between them filled with everything they couldn't say.

"I'll be ready," he said, his voice steady. "But I need you to do something for me."

Ixchel wiped her eyes, trying to stay strong. "Anything," she whispered.

"After the ritual... after it's done... I want you to lead our people. They will need you."

Her heart clenched. "I'm not a leader, Balam. I'm just—"

"You are more than you know," he interrupted, his hand brushing her cheek. "You are the reason we've made it this far. The gods chose you, too."

THE DAWN OF THE JAGUAR

She looked into his eyes, searching for any hint of fear, but all she saw was acceptance. He had come to terms with his fate, but she hadn't. Not yet.

"I don't want to say goodbye," she whispered, her voice trembling.

Balam leaned forward, pressing his forehead gently against hers. "Then don't. I'll always be with you, Ixchel. In the stars, in the wind, in the very heart of Yax Mutal. You will never be alone."

Tears fell freely now, and Ixchel closed her eyes, savoring the warmth of his touch. Tomorrow, that warmth would be gone. Tomorrow, the gods would take him from her.

But tonight, for just a little longer, he was still hers.

They stayed like that for a moment, suspended in time, until Balam pulled away, his eyes filled with both sorrow and peace.

"It's time," he whispered, and with those words, the final chapter of their story began to unfold.

Chapter 26: The Final Offering

The first light of dawn crept over the horizon, casting a soft, golden glow over Yax Mutal. The city was eerily quiet, the usual hum of daily life replaced by a heavy silence that hung in the air like a funeral shroud. No one moved through the streets; no voices called out in greeting. The people of Yax Mutal knew what was coming, and they waited, breath held, for the moment when their king would make the ultimate sacrifice.

High atop the Great Pyramid, preparations for the ritual were underway. Priests dressed in ceremonial robes, their faces painted with the symbols of the gods, moved with slow, deliberate steps. The air was thick with the scent of burning copal, the fragrant smoke rising in swirling patterns toward the sky, as if carrying prayers to the heavens.

Balam stood at the edge of the pyramid, his eyes scanning the city below. His people were waiting. He could feel their presence, even though he could not see them. They were with him, just as he was with them, in this final act. The jaguar god, whose power he had felt coursing through him on the battlefield, now demanded his life in exchange for peace.

Beside him, Ixchel stood quietly, her heart a storm of emotions. She had been preparing for this moment, steeling herself for what was to come, but now, standing so close to the end, she felt her resolve waver. The gods had chosen Balam, and his fate was sealed, but that didn't make it any easier to bear. She had seen it all in her visions—the victory, the peace, the sacrifice—but she had never truly understood the weight of what it meant until now.

The head priest, Ah Kin Chi, approached, his face solemn beneath the weight of his own role. "It is time, my king," he said, his voice low and respectful.

Balam nodded, turning toward the altar where the ritual would take place. His steps were steady, his face calm. He had accepted his fate, and now he would see it through.

Ixchel walked beside him, her hands clenched tightly at her sides. She had promised herself she wouldn't cry, wouldn't let her emotions break through in front of Balam, but the tears threatened to spill over anyway. How could she stand here, watching the man who had become so much more than a leader, a warrior, or a king, walk toward his death? How could she let him go?

As they reached the altar, Balam stopped and turned to face her. For a long moment, they simply looked at each other, the unspoken words between them heavy in the air.

"Ixchel," Balam said softly, his voice breaking through the silence. "You know what comes next."

She nodded, unable to trust her voice.

"Do not grieve for me," he continued. "This is what the gods demand. This is what will save Yax Mutal."

"But why you?" Ixchel whispered, her voice trembling with the weight of the question. "Why must it be you?"

Balam smiled, a sad, weary smile that held the wisdom of a man who had seen too much in too little time. "The gods always take the best of us. It has always been this way. And in the end, Ixchel, it was never about just one person. It is about the city, about the people. They are what matters. We are merely the instruments of the gods."

Ixchel's throat tightened as she fought to hold back her tears. "I don't want to lose you."

"You won't," Balam said softly. "I will always be here. In the land, in the sky, in the heart of Yax Mutal. And you... you will lead them now."

She shook her head, her voice breaking. "I'm not ready."

Balam reached out and took her hands in his. "You are ready. You've been ready for this moment since the gods first gave you your

THE DAWN OF THE JAGUAR

visions. You've always been stronger than you know, Ixchel. And now, the people will look to you. They will need you."

The weight of his words settled over her like a mantle. She had never wanted this—this burden of leadership, of prophecy, of the future of Yax Mutal resting on her shoulders. But now, with Balam standing before her, on the brink of his own end, she realized that she had no choice. The gods had chosen her just as much as they had chosen him.

With a final, trembling breath, Ixchel nodded. "I will do it," she whispered. "For you. For the city."

Balam smiled again, and this time there was peace in his eyes. "Thank you."

The moment stretched between them, a fragile, bittersweet pause before the inevitable. Then, with a deep breath, Balam turned toward the altar.

Ah Kin Chi, the head priest, began chanting the sacred prayers, his voice rising and falling in a rhythmic cadence that seemed to vibrate through the very stones of the pyramid. The other priests joined in, their voices weaving together in a powerful chorus, calling upon the gods to witness the sacrifice that was about to be made.

Balam knelt before the altar, his head bowed in submission to the divine will. Ah Kin Chi approached, holding the ceremonial blade in his hands, its obsidian edge gleaming in the early morning light. The moment had come.

Ixchel's heart pounded in her chest as she watched, every fiber of her being screaming against what was about to happen. But she stood still, knowing that this was what had to be done. The gods had spoken, and now the city's fate rested on this final act.

Ah Kin Chi raised the blade high, his voice rising in a final, powerful invocation to the gods. And then, in one swift, merciful motion, the blade descended.

The world seemed to stop. For a moment, there was only silence, the kind of deep, all-encompassing silence that fills the air just before a storm. And then, the sky above Yax Mutal darkened, as if the gods themselves were mourning the loss of the king.

Balam's body lay still upon the altar, his face peaceful in death. The jaguar god had claimed him, and with that, the prophecy was fulfilled.

Ixchel stood frozen, her heart shattering in her chest. She had known this moment was coming, had seen it in her visions, but the reality of it was so much more than she could bear. Tears streamed down her face, silent and unbidden, as she gazed at the man she had come to love more deeply than she had ever thought possible.

The priests continued their chants, their voices rising in a mournful song that echoed across the city. Below, the people of Yax Mutal gathered, their heads bowed in respect and sorrow for their fallen king. They had won the war, but at a terrible cost.

The jaguar god had spared their city, but Yax Mutal was left in mourning.

As the sun began to rise, casting its golden light over the pyramid and the city below, Ixchel wiped her tears and took a deep breath. She knew what she had to do now. She would lead them, just as Balam had asked. She would honor his sacrifice by ensuring that Yax Mutal thrived, that the peace he had given his life for would endure.

She would not fail him.

With one last, lingering look at Balam, Ixchel turned and walked down the steps of the pyramid, her head held high. The people watched her, their eyes filled with hope and grief, knowing that she was now their leader, their guide.

The gods had taken Balam, but they had given Yax Mutal a future.

And Ixchel would make sure it was one worth living.

Chapter 27: Shadows of the Past

The golden rays of the morning sun streamed through the dense canopy of the jungle surrounding Yax Mutal, casting long shadows over the towering temples and bustling plazas below. Life had returned to the city after the long, brutal war. Where once there had been mourning and despair, there was now hope and renewal. Merchants bartered in the marketplace, children laughed as they played near the Sacred Cenote, and the priests performed their rituals to the gods with a newfound fervor.

But while the city thrived, Ixchel remained a solitary figure, standing atop the Great Pyramid where Balam had made his final sacrifice. She looked out over the city, her heart heavy despite the outward signs of prosperity. The people called her the chosen one, the priestess of the jaguar god, the voice of the gods themselves, but none of those titles brought her comfort. She could still see Balam's face in her mind, could still hear his final words as he prepared to give his life for Yax Mutal.

The weight of that memory pressed down on her, as constant and unrelenting as the midday heat.

Below her, the plaza was filled with people preparing for a celebration. It had been a full cycle of the calendar since the war ended, and the city was honoring its newfound peace with a festival. Brightly colored banners fluttered in the breeze, and offerings of food and flowers were placed on altars to thank the gods for their mercy.

Yet, despite the joy and laughter echoing through the streets, Ixchel felt only emptiness.

Her footsteps echoed lightly on the stone steps of the pyramid as she descended, her ceremonial robes flowing behind her like a shadow. The people below turned to look at her, bowing their heads in reverence as she passed. They whispered her name with a mixture of awe and fear, their eyes following her every move. To them, she was more than a leader now—she was the one who had communed with the gods, who had seen the future, who had carried them through the darkest of times.

To Ixchel, she was simply a woman grieving for the man she had loved.

As she walked through the plaza, a young girl ran up to her, holding a bundle of flowers in her tiny hands. "Priestess Ixchel," the girl said, her voice soft but full of excitement. "These are for you. To thank you for saving us."

Ixchel knelt down, forcing a smile as she took the flowers from the girl's outstretched hands. "Thank you, little one," she said gently, her fingers brushing over the delicate petals. "But it is the gods who saved us. I only followed their will."

The girl's eyes widened in awe. "But you spoke to them! You are their voice!"

Ixchel's smile faltered for a moment. "Yes," she said quietly. "I spoke to them."

The girl giggled and ran off, leaving Ixchel standing alone with the flowers. She watched the child disappear into the crowd, a deep ache forming in her chest. The people saw her as a symbol of their survival, but they didn't know the price she had paid. They didn't know what she had lost. No one did.

Her thoughts were interrupted by the approach of Ah Kin Chi, the head priest who had overseen the ritual of Balam's sacrifice. His face was lined with age and wisdom, his eyes filled with understanding as he came to stand beside her.

"You have been quiet today, Ixchel," Ah Kin Chi said, his voice low and respectful. "The people are celebrating, but you seem distant."

THE DAWN OF THE JAGUAR

Ixchel sighed, her gaze fixed on the horizon. "I feel... lost," she admitted softly. "I did what the gods asked of me. I fulfilled the prophecy. But now that it's over, I don't know where I belong."

Ah Kin Chi nodded, his eyes thoughtful. "It is not uncommon to feel such things after great trials. The gods ask much of those they choose. But you have given the people hope, Ixchel. You have brought peace."

"Peace," Ixchel repeated, the word tasting bitter on her tongue. "But at what cost? Balam is gone. He gave everything for this city, and now..."

"Now you carry the burden of his memory," Ah Kin Chi said gently. "That is the way of things. The gods take, and they give. They took Balam, but they have given you life, and with it, the responsibility to guide our people."

Ixchel turned to look at him, her eyes filled with sorrow. "I don't know if I can do it. I am haunted by what I've seen, by what I've lost. Every night, I dream of him. I see his face, hear his voice. He is with me, but always just out of reach."

The priest's face softened with compassion. "Grief is a powerful force, but it need not consume you. Balam's spirit is with the gods now, watching over us all. And you... you are still here. Your journey is not over."

Ixchel clenched her fists, the weight of her grief pressing down on her like a heavy stone. "I miss him," she whispered, her voice breaking. "Every moment, I miss him."

"I know," Ah Kin Chi said softly. "But the gods chose you for a reason. They saw something in you, something strong enough to bear this burden. You must trust in their wisdom, even when it feels unbearable."

For a long moment, Ixchel said nothing. The weight of Ah Kin Chi's words hung in the air, mixing with the sounds of the festival around them. She knew he was right—the gods had chosen her for this path, and she could not turn away from it. But knowing that didn't make it any easier to bear.

Finally, she looked up at the sky, where the sun had risen to its highest point, bathing the city in its warm glow. "I will try," she said quietly. "For the people. For Balam."

Ah Kin Chi smiled, a small but encouraging smile. "That is all the gods ask of us."

As the priest turned to leave, Ixchel stood alone once more, her thoughts still heavy but her heart a little lighter. She had been chosen by the gods to lead, and though the weight of her grief would never fully leave her, she knew now that she could not let it define her.

The people needed her, just as they had needed Balam. And she would not fail them.

As the day wore on and the festival reached its peak, Ixchel walked among the people, speaking to them, blessing their offerings, and listening to their stories. Though her heart still ached with the loss of Balam, she found strength in the faces of those she served. They looked to her with trust and faith, believing that she would lead them into a future of peace and prosperity.

And so, with each step she took, Ixchel began to see her place in this new world. She was no longer just the girl from a small village, no longer just the one who saw visions. She was their leader now, the chosen one of the gods, and she would carry that mantle with honor, just as Balam had carried his.

As night fell and the city of Yax Mutal glowed with the light of a thousand torches, Ixchel stood atop the Great Pyramid once more, looking out over the city she had saved.

The gods were appeased. The people were safe.

And though her heart still carried the weight of loss, she knew that Balam's spirit was with her, guiding her forward.

For the first time in what felt like an eternity, she allowed herself a small, bittersweet smile.

THE DAWN OF THE JAGUAR

The future of Yax Mutal was bright, and she would lead them into it.

Chapter 28: The Weight of Peace

The smoke of battle had long since drifted into the jungle, leaving behind only memories of the chaos that had nearly consumed Yax Mutal. Calakmul's armies had retreated, their banners torn, their warriors humbled. The once-great threat that loomed over the city like a storm cloud was now no more than a distant shadow on the horizon. Peace had returned, though not without a price.

Ixchel stood atop the Great Pyramid, as she often did in moments of deep contemplation, watching the tranquil city below. The rhythm of everyday life had resumed; farmers tilled their fields, merchants haggled over goods, and children played near the temple steps. The sounds of the city—familiar and comforting—filled the air, yet Ixchel felt a strange hollowness beneath it all.

Peace. A word that had once seemed so elusive now surrounded her like the warm embrace of the jungle, yet she could not help but feel the weight of its cost.

A soft rustle behind her broke her reverie. It was Ah Kin Chi, the elderly priest who had guided her throughout these trials. His footsteps were light, his presence calming.

"Priestess," he said, his voice barely more than a whisper in the wind. "The council is waiting for your guidance on the next steps for the city."

Ixchel did not turn to face him immediately. Her gaze remained on the city, her mind distant. "They are expecting me to lead them into a new era," she said quietly, her voice carrying a heaviness that echoed her thoughts. "But what if I lead them astray? What if this peace is nothing more than an illusion, born of blood and sacrifice?"

Ah Kin Chi stepped closer, his old eyes following hers as he looked over Yax Mutal. "Peace is always bought with sacrifice," he replied. "The gods ask for much, and they give much in return. But that does not mean the peace we now have is false."

Ixchel sighed. "I know that, in my mind. But my heart..." She placed a hand over her chest, where the weight of her grief and doubt seemed to press hardest. "My heart cannot forget what we've lost. Balam, my father, the countless lives taken in battle. Was it truly the will of the gods that so many should die? And for what? For a peace that might not last?"

The priest was silent for a moment, considering her words. Then, with a gentle smile, he said, "The gods do not always reveal their full plans to us. We mortals can only see a small part of their design. But Balam... he gave his life for this peace. He believed in it. And the people believe in you, Ixchel."

"I'm not sure I believe in myself anymore," she admitted, her voice trembling. "I was chosen by the gods, but all I feel now is doubt. Did I make the right choices? Did I honor Balam's memory? Or did I simply fulfill a prophecy that was beyond my control?"

Ah Kin Chi reached out and placed a hand on her shoulder, his grip firm but kind. "You have borne a great burden, Ixchel. It is natural to question. But know this: peace was not given to you, nor was it simply a gift of the gods. It was earned. Through your strength, through your vision, through the sacrifices you made. This peace belongs to you as much as it does to the gods."

Ixchel closed her eyes, letting the old priest's words wash over her. She wanted to believe him, to accept that the peace Yax Mutal now enjoyed was something she had helped create. But the memories of Balam's sacrifice haunted her still, along with the haunting images from her visions. She had seen the gods intervene in ways she could not fully understand, and the cost of that divine interference was always paid in mortal lives.

"I fear that the gods will ask for more," she whispered, opening her eyes again to look at the horizon, where the jungle met the sky. "That this peace is only temporary, and that one day, they will demand more blood to maintain it."

Ah Kin Chi's grip on her shoulder tightened slightly, a comforting presence amidst her inner turmoil. "Perhaps they will," he said softly. "But that is not something you can control. The gods have their ways, but so do we. You have the power to lead these people, Ixchel. You have shown them that they can survive even the worst of storms. And you have the wisdom to guide them forward, not as a mere instrument of the gods, but as a leader in your own right."

His words struck something deep within her. She had always seen herself as a vessel for the gods' will, as someone chosen to interpret their desires for the people. But now, for the first time, she considered the possibility that her role was not just to serve the gods but to lead her people in her own way. The gods had chosen her, yes, but that did not mean she had no agency.

Finally, she turned to Ah Kin Chi, her face softer, though the grief still lingered in her eyes. "Thank you," she said, her voice steadier now. "You have always known the right words to say."

The priest smiled, his weathered face crinkling with warmth. "It is not wisdom, merely experience. I have lived through many trials, but none so great as these. And yet, here we are."

Ixchel nodded, taking a deep breath. "The people will need guidance, not just from the gods, but from me. I must find the strength to carry on, for them."

"Indeed," Ah Kin Chi agreed. "And you will. You already have."

As the sun began to dip toward the horizon, casting a golden light over the city, Ixchel felt a sense of resolve settle over her. She had been through so much—loss, sacrifice, war—and now she stood on the other side of it, scarred but stronger. The gods had demanded much, and she had given it, but now she would lead Yax Mutal not as a mere servant of fate, but as its guide.

"I will speak to the council," she said, her voice more certain now. "I will tell them that we must rebuild, not just the city but ourselves. This peace is fragile, and we must cherish it, protect it. But we must also move forward. We cannot live in fear of the gods' next demand."

Ah Kin Chi smiled, bowing his head slightly. "That is wise, Ixchel. The people will follow you. They believe in you."

"And I will believe in them," she replied.

As she walked back toward the temple steps, the weight of her doubts still lingered, but there was something else now—a sense of purpose, of clarity. She was no longer just a priestess interpreting the will of distant gods. She was a leader, one who would forge a new path for her people, with or without the gods' intervention.

For the first time in a long while, Ixchel felt the stirrings of hope in her heart.

The future of Yax Mutal lay not just in the hands of the gods, but in the hands of its people. And she would be there to guide them, every step of the way.

Chapter 29: The Eternal Guardian

The night was thick with silence. From the heights of the Great Pyramid, Ixchel stood looking out over the city of Yax Mutal. The stars twinkled dimly, as though they too were weary from the long struggle that had consumed the land. She had not slept for days, the burden of her role weighing heavier than ever. The people saw her now as their spiritual leader, a beacon in the darkness, yet inside, she felt hollow.

The death of Balam, the prince, the warrior, the one who had given everything for their city, had left a wound in her heart that no power could heal. His sacrifice had brought peace to Yax Mutal, but the cost was greater than she had ever imagined. Even now, the drums of mourning still echoed faintly in the streets, as the city honored the fallen—both their king and their new ruler.

Ixchel pressed her hand to her chest, the faint glow of the moon reflecting off her tear-streaked face. "Balam," she whispered into the wind, her voice trembling. "Where are you now?"

The air around her felt heavier, the ancient stones beneath her feet vibrating with the energy of the gods. The very night seemed to pulse with a deeper meaning, one she had come to understand in her visions. She knew something was coming—something beyond the veil of the mortal world. She could feel the gods stirring, their presence brushing against the edge of her awareness.

And then, the vision came.

The world around her shifted, the familiar skyline of Yax Mutal dissolving into golden mist. She was no longer atop the Great Pyramid. She stood instead on a wide, open plain that stretched far into the distance, bordered by towering jungle trees that rustled with an unseen wind. The air was warm here, filled with the scents of earth and fire, and the sky above burned with the deep red hues of twilight.

Before her, the temple loomed, larger and grander than any she had ever seen. It glowed faintly with an otherworldly light, as though it were alive. She felt herself drawn toward it, her feet moving of their own accord as she approached the base of the grand steps. Her heart pounded in her chest, the air around her growing thick with tension. The presence of the gods was palpable here.

Then, from the shadows beneath the temple steps, a figure emerged. Balam.

Ixchel gasped, her breath catching in her throat. He was different now—taller, more imposing. His skin gleamed with a faint golden glow, and the markings of the jaguar god were etched across his chest and arms. His eyes glowed softly in the dim light, filled with the wisdom of the divine. He was not merely the Balam she had known, but something more—an eternal guardian, a part of the divine that now watched over Yax Mutal.

"Balam..." she whispered, her voice fragile. "Is it really you?"

He smiled at her, that same soft smile that had always brought her comfort, though now there was an otherworldly calm in his expression. "Ixchel," he said, his voice deep and gentle, like the rustling of the wind through the trees. "You have come."

Tears welled up in her eyes as she took a tentative step forward. "I've been waiting... waiting to see you again. To understand what happened. You're... you're one with the gods now."

Balam nodded, his gaze never leaving hers. "The jaguar god and I are one, bound by the sacrifice I made. It was always my destiny, though neither of us could see it clearly before."

She shook her head, tears spilling down her cheeks. "But I didn't want this. I never wanted you to leave us... to leave me. How can I carry on without you?"

THE DAWN OF THE JAGUAR

He stepped closer, the air around him warm and comforting, like the embrace of the jungle. "Ixchel, you were never alone. The gods have always been with you, guiding your path, and you—more than anyone—have the strength to lead our people now. You have been chosen."

Her voice broke, the weight of her sorrow overwhelming her. "I don't know if I can do it," she confessed. "The people look to me for guidance, for answers, but without you... I don't know if I'm enough."

Balam's eyes softened, and he reached out, though his hand never truly touched her. Still, she could feel the warmth of his presence, the comfort of his belief in her. "Ixchel, you were always more than enough. You led our people through the darkest times. You saw what others could not, and you had the courage to follow your visions. That was not the work of the gods alone—it was your strength, your wisdom."

His words settled into her heart, like seeds waiting to bloom. She had always questioned her role, her visions, the destiny that had been thrust upon her. But Balam had believed in her, and now, standing before him, she could feel that same belief stirring within herself.

"But what about you?" she asked, her voice trembling. "What will happen to you now?"

Balam turned, his gaze drifting toward the distant temple that glowed with the light of the divine. "I will remain here," he said softly. "I will watch over Yax Mutal, as I always have. The jaguar god and I are bound to the city, to its people. I will protect them, even in death."

Ixchel's heart ached at his words, but she understood now. He was no longer just the prince she had loved—he had become something greater, a part of the city's very soul. He would watch over them, from the shadows of the divine realm, for all eternity.

"Will I ever see you again?" she whispered, her voice barely audible.

Balam smiled, his eyes filled with infinite tenderness. "I will always be with you, Ixchel. In every breath of wind, in every flicker of flame.

You will feel my presence, even if you do not see me. And when your time comes, we will meet again."

She nodded, though the pain of his absence still cut deep. She knew now that her path was not to follow him into the afterlife, but to lead Yax Mutal into its future. The gods had chosen her, and Balam's faith in her had given her the strength to accept that role.

As the vision began to fade, the golden mist swirling around her, Ixchel took one last look at Balam. He stood tall and proud, the jaguar god's guardian, watching over the city he had given everything to protect.

"Until we meet again," she whispered, her voice filled with love and sorrow.

And then, he was gone.

The world returned to the quiet stillness of the temple, the stars blinking faintly overhead. But Ixchel no longer felt alone. She carried Balam with her now, his presence etched into her soul, a part of her just as he had become a part of the gods.

She stood tall, her heart lighter than it had been in many moons. The future of Yax Mutal was in her hands, and though the path ahead was uncertain, she knew that Balam—her eternal guardian—would watch over them all.

And with that, she stepped forward, ready to lead her people into a new dawn.

Chapter 30: A New Dawn

The first rays of the sun broke over the horizon, casting a golden light over the city of Yax Mutal. From the top of the Great Pyramid, Ixchel stood in silence, watching as the city below slowly came to life. The stone buildings glowed in the early light, the shadows of the past night melting away in the warmth of the dawn. Birds flew overhead, their songs rising like prayers to the gods. The air was still, carrying the scent of rain and earth from the jungles beyond the city.

It had been months since Balam's sacrifice, months of rebuilding, mourning, and healing. The jaguar god had been appeased, and Yax Mutal, once on the brink of destruction, had found peace again. But that peace had come at a cost—a cost Ixchel still carried in her heart every day.

"Are you ready?" a voice asked from behind her.

Ixchel turned to see Nah Kan, one of the elders who had remained loyal to the city through the darkest of times. He was a man of few words but wise beyond measure, his eyes reflecting the history of generations past.

She nodded slowly. "As ready as I will ever be."

Today was a day of new beginnings, but also of remembrance. The city was preparing for the ceremony that would mark Ixchel's official rise as the spiritual leader, a role she had not sought but one she knew she could not refuse. The people looked to her now, not just for guidance, but as a symbol of the gods' will. She had become their beacon, the living embodiment of the balance between the human and the divine.

Nah Kan came to stand beside her, his hands resting on the stone balustrade. "The people trust you, Ixchel. They see the strength in you that Balam saw. They will follow you."

"But will they understand?" she asked quietly, her eyes drifting back to the city. "They honor Balam as their hero, their king, but they do not know the burden he carried. They don't know the sacrifice he made."

Nah Kan was silent for a moment, his gaze steady. "It is not for them to know the full weight of what you and Balam carried. They see what they need to see—a protector, a leader. They see the city that still stands because of him. And because of you."

The words soothed her, though the ache in her heart remained. She had not seen Balam in her visions since that final encounter by the cenote. But she felt him everywhere. In the wind, in the stars, in the quiet moments when the city slept. She knew he was watching, just as he had promised.

"Come," Nah Kan said, his voice gentle but firm. "It is time."

They descended the steps of the pyramid together, the cool stone beneath their feet a reminder of the generations that had come before them. Below, the plaza was filled with people—men, women, children, all gathered in anticipation of the ceremony. It was a sea of colors, the people dressed in their finest garments, with feathers and jade adorning their hair and clothes. The air hummed with expectation.

As Ixchel and Nah Kan reached the base of the pyramid, the crowd parted to let them through. There were whispers, murmurs of awe and respect, and Ixchel could feel the weight of their gazes on her. These were the people she was meant to lead, the people who had fought for their city, who had suffered and survived. She had once been one of them, an ordinary girl from a village far from the grandeur of Yax Mutal. Now, she was their protector.

At the center of the plaza stood the sacred altar, draped in white cloth and adorned with offerings to the gods—fruits, flowers, and incense. The scent of copal filled the air, rising in thick, fragrant clouds that seemed to reach toward the heavens. The high priest stood beside the altar, his face painted with the sacred colors of the jaguar god, his eyes closed in prayer.

THE DAWN OF THE JAGUAR

As Ixchel approached, the priest opened his eyes and looked at her with deep reverence. He nodded, stepping aside to allow her to take her place before the altar. She stood there, her heart pounding in her chest, the weight of her new role pressing down on her shoulders.

But then, as the sun rose higher in the sky, a calmness settled over her. She closed her eyes and breathed in the scent of the earth, the jungle, the life all around her. She remembered the vision of Balam, his presence a steady warmth in her soul.

The priest raised his hands to the sky, and the crowd fell silent.

"Today, we honor the gods," he said, his voice strong and clear. "We honor their protection, their guidance, and the sacrifices made in their name. Our city stands because of the balance between the human and the divine, between the earth and the heavens."

He turned to Ixchel, his gaze filled with solemnity. "Ixchel, chosen by the gods, you have walked the path they set before you. You have seen what others could not, and you have carried the burden of that knowledge. Today, we ask you to take your place as the spiritual protector of Yax Mutal. Do you accept this duty?"

Ixchel opened her eyes, feeling the weight of the moment. She looked out at the faces of her people, at the city that had been saved by Balam's sacrifice, by the jaguar god's mercy. She thought of her journey, of the visions that had led her here, and of the responsibility that now rested in her hands.

"I accept," she said, her voice steady and strong.

The priest nodded, raising his hands once more. "Then let the gods bear witness."

The crowd erupted in cheers, their voices rising like a great wave of sound that echoed across the city. Ixchel stood tall, her heart filled with both sorrow and hope. She knew that the path ahead would not be easy. There would be challenges, both from within and without. But she also knew that she was not alone.

As the ceremony continued, Ixchel felt a warmth settle over her, a presence that she knew could only be Balam. She closed her eyes for a moment, her lips curving into a soft smile.

"I will not fail you," she whispered.

The sun climbed higher in the sky, its light shining brightly over Yax Mutal. The city had survived, and now, it was ready to face whatever the future held. As the people celebrated, Ixchel stood quietly, watching over them as Balam once had. She was their protector now, their guide.

And as the sun bathed the city in its golden light, she knew that the dawn of a new era had begun.

Don't miss out!

Visit the website below and you can sign up to receive emails whenever Anupam Roy publishes a new book. There's no charge and no obligation.

https://books2read.com/r/B-A-UKBS-XWRBF

BOOKS 2 READ

Connecting independent readers to independent writers.

Did you love *The Dawn of the Jaguar*? Then you should read *The Empire of the Sun: An Incan Chronicle*[1] by Anupam Roy!

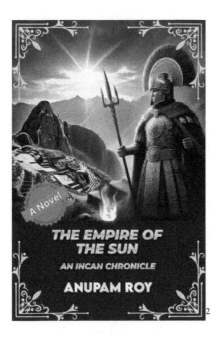

Book Description: *The Empire of the Sun: An Incan Chronicle*

Set against the breathtaking backdrop of the Inca Empire at its height, ***The Empire of the Sun: An Incan Chronicle*** is an epic tale of love, power, and destiny. Spanning the vast landscapes of ancient Tawantinsuyu—from the sacred capital of Cusco to the mystical shores of Lake Titicaca—this novel brings to life a world where gods walk among men and rulers are chosen by the heavens.

At the heart of the story is Tupac Yupanqui, a prince born to the mighty Sapa Inca Pachacuti, destined to inherit a vast empire. Trained as both a warrior and a leader, Tupac faces the challenges of internal strife and external rebellions, as he learns the heavy cost of power.

---

1. https://books2read.com/u/baygp8

2. https://books2read.com/u/baygp8

Alongside him is Mama Quilla, a humble commoner and skilled healer whose intelligence and compassion draw her into the heart of the empire's political intrigues. Their fates are intertwined by prophecy, but they must navigate the deep divide between their social stations, even as their bond grows stronger.

As civil war threatens to tear the empire apart and enemies rise both within and beyond its borders, Tupac must confront his own brother in a deadly battle for the future of the Inca. Meanwhile, Mama Quilla finds herself at the crossroads of personal sacrifice and the welfare of her people, drawn into a conflict far larger than she ever imagined.

Blending historical elements with mythology, ***The Empire of the Sun: An Incan Chronicle*** explores themes of leadership, sacrifice, and the eternal struggle between duty and desire. With richly drawn characters and a sweeping narrative, the novel offers a glimpse into the complexity of Incan society, where commoners and nobles, warriors and priests, are united under the divine mandate of the gods but divided by the ever-present forces of ambition and love.

For readers who love historical epics, ***The Empire of the Sun: An Incan Chronicle*** is a poignant and immersive journey into the heart of one of the most fascinating civilizations in history—a tale of empires built and broken, and the people who rise and fall within them.

Also by Anupam Roy

American Heroes
The Heroes of American Freedom Movements: A Glimpse of American History

A Study in Scarlet: Annotated
Sir Arthur Conan Doyle's A Study in Scarlet: Annotated

Christmas Story Time
Christmas Stories
Christmas Stories
Christmas Stories Volume 3

Ghost Stories
Ghost Stories
The Archivist's Curse

Greek Mythology

Greek Mythology, Volume 1

Greek Mythology: A Teen's Version
Greek Mythology: A Teen's Version

Happy Easter Story Anthology
Happy Easter Volume 1
The Easter Bunny's Secret
Chronicles of The Easter Bunny

I'm Maya And It's My Story
I'm Maya And It's My Story

The Adventures of Alex Mercer
The Midnight Mansion Mystery

The Adventures of Zoro
The Adventures of Zoro: The Rise of North Brook

The Toy Kingdom
The Toy Kingdom Volume 1
The Toy Kingdom Volume 2
The Toy Kingdom Volume 3

The Toyoearth
The Toyoearth Volume 1

Valentine's Day Love Stories
Valentine's Day Love Stories Volume 1
Valentine's Day in Venice
The Love Locket
Chasing Fireflies

Valentine's Day Mystery Anthology
Love's Mysterious Embrace
Roses and Riddles
Enigmatic Hearts

Warrior Chronicles
Napoleon Bonaparte: The Enigma Unveiled
Alexander
Joan of Arc: Unveiling the Untold Secrets

Standalone
How to Increase Confidence and Be Successful
Unlock Your True Potential
A Comprehensive Guide to Yacht Maintenance
✧✧✧✧✧ ✧✧✧✧ - Towards Light

Unlock the Secret to the Most Magical Christmas Ever! Unique Celebrations Await!
New Year Resolutions: Look Before You Leap
Christmas Stories Omnibus
New Year, New You: A Holistic Approach to Personal Growth
Financial Fitness for the New Year
The Wealth Mindset Blueprint
Valentine's Day Love Stories
Happy Saint Patrick's Day
Happy Easter Story Anthology
The Last Supper
From Startup to Scaleup: The Entrepreneur's Playbook for Growth and Impact
The Stories on St. George's Day
The Symphony of the Sea
The Beat of Our Hearts
Forbidden Juneteenth Love
The Story of American Independence: A Journey to Freedom
The Power of Action: Unlocking the Path to Success
The Long Game
The Bluebone Pirates
The Empire of the Sun: An Incan Chronicle
The Dawn of the Jaguar

About the Author

Anupam Roy, born on January 6, 1982, in the serene town of Kalna, Burdwan district, West Bengal, India, is a distinguished poet and author based in Murshidabad, near Kolkata, in India. His academic journey led him to the esteemed University of Burdwan, where he pursued a Master of Arts in English, a discipline that would become the canvas for his storytelling.

Literature is Anupam Roy's first love, and it serves as his medium for connecting with the human experience and delving into the intricate tapestry of human emotions. He has authored numerous books, each a testament to his literary prowess and his ability to encapsulate the essence of human existence. His writing is characterized by lyrical beauty, evocative imagery, and keen observation, often transforming everyday moments into poetic expressions that explore the complexities of human relationships.

Beyond his literary pursuits, Anupam Roy is a revered figure in West Bengal's literary circles and beyond. His work transcends cultural boundaries, resonating with readers from diverse backgrounds, a testament to the universality of his themes and the depth of his insights.

Anupam Roy's writing often delves into the profound connection between nature and human existence, celebrating the beauty of the natural world while exploring the depths of human emotions. His eloquent words and poignant storytelling continue to inspire and captivate readers, leaving an indelible mark in the world of Indian literature.

An ongoing exploration of the human condition, Anupam Roy's literary journey invites readers to embark on a voyage of self-discovery and reflection through the power of literature. His ability to convey life's complexities in simple yet profound terms solidifies his status as a cherished figure in Indian literature, touching the hearts and minds of those privileged to read his work.

Milton Keynes UK
Ingram Content Group UK Ltd.
UKHW040256181024
449757UK00001B/67